GUILTY?

A Swedish Crime Novel

Stockholm Sleuth Series
(Book 4)

Christer Tholin

ISBN: 978-91-985795-7-4 (pocketbook)
ISBN: 978-91-985796-7-3 (mobi eBook)

For my mother

CONTENT

Your Free Book

Read the Prequel to the Stockholm Sleuth Series

A short crime story about Lars, one of the private eyes in the series. In this story he is still working as a policeman.
Together with his partner Kalle, Lars is called to a house where neighbours report a quarrel.
This case will change Lars' career forever.

Exclusive short story for readers of the series – download here:

www.christertholin.one/free

PART I

April 2018

1

It was the first day after Easter vacation. She went about her morning as usual, still blissfully unaware that this would be the day that would change her life forever. During the midday break, before eating lunch, she went outside the school with Klara to get some fresh air.

Her friend was the first to notice him. "Hey, check out that guy over there. Isn't he cute?"

His car was in the parking lot out in front of the school, the boy was leaning under the propped open car hood and was tinkering on the engine.

Hanna looked over and was immediately mesmerized. His muscles and how they would flex under his shirt, the way he moved. They both just stood there spellbound.

After some time, Hanna noticed that he was throwing glances in their direction at them. Her first thought was that he was interested in Klara, because everyone always only wanted Klara. No wonder, because Klara was a lot prettier than she was. Klara had a slim, but feminine, figure with quite a rack. She, on the other hand, was more on the skinny side and her breasts were virtually invisible under her t-shirt. Fortunately, push-up bras were a thing and so she could at least give the impression as if she had some. And her face lacked any sort of definition, it was not as beautifully contoured as Klara's. And then there were those ridiculous freckles and acne. Without makeup, nobody would ever even look at her. To make matters worse, she couldn't keep up with Klara in terms of stylish clothes either. She did not have the same financial resources. However, Klara often gave her something. Otherwise she wouldn't have anything decent to wear.

"How old do you think he is?"

Klara pursed her small mouth. "Well, he has to be at least 18, otherwise he wouldn't even be allowed to drive. Maybe 19 or 20?"

Hanna nodded. Just then, he once again looked over. Yes, he really was looking at her. Hanna blushed and turned towards Klara. They whispered to each other and continued to observe the cute boy. After a while he wiped off his hands and came towards them. Hanna wanted to sink into the ground and if Klara had not been there, she would have tried to leave.

He introduced himself politely. "Hello, you two lovely ladies. My name is Ali. Maybe you can help me? I'm having a problem with my car and I need a spare part to get it running again. I have to go to Solna for that. I don't usually take the bus, so I am not really familiar with it. How do I get there?"

Hanna just stared at him and couldn't get a word out. Klara, on the other hand, batted her eyelashes and explained to him how to get to the Sundbyberg subway station. While he listened to Klara, Ali kept glancing over at Hanna and looked deep into her eyes. Hanna knew that her face was bright red, which made the situation even more embarrassing for her. Finally, he said goodbye. Not just with a simple "*hejdå*", but he also shook hands with them both. Hanna just barely managed to give him her hand and he held it for a moment, a moment that seemed more like several minutes to her. One part of her found it wonderful to hold his hand, but another part of her felt the need to break free and run away. Needless to say, she remained where she was, completely frozen in place, and looked at him as if in a trance as he walked away towards the subway station.

Klara nudged her. "Hey, are you in a coma? What is the matter with you?"

Hanna slowly came back to reality. "Oh, nothing. Let's go back."

Klara of course immediately realized what was going on with her and teased her all day long about it. Hanna could hardly concentrate on her classes after lunch anyway, she had to constantly think of Ali, how he had looked at her and how he had held her hand - firmly and tenderly at the same time. After school, she made a beeline for the parking lot to check on Ali's car, but it was no longer there. Disappointed, she headed home.

***

The knocking woke her up. "Get up. You still have half an hour; I have to go now." The shrill voice of her mother.

"All right." Damn it, had she not heard the alarm go off? She reached for her smartphone. Shit, she'd forgotten to set the alarm. It was already 7:00. She had to be at the subway station no later than 7:30. With great effort she managed to sit up. The week was off to a great start. She had already had enough of it. She swung one leg out of bed, but then she laid down again. She would skip the first two hours of school. It was only gym class – she just happened to have her period. She'd forge her mother's signature.

She snuggled back into the blanket and closed her eyes again for a while. She didn't want this life anymore. It was all so boring. She just wanted to be with Ali. Even if she had only known him for a week. She thought of his deep dark brown eyes and his tender hands. And that charming smile, he had such beautiful teeth. She still couldn't believe that he was interested in her at all.

After their first meeting together, she had feared that she would never see him again. But then he had been there again the next day as they were coming out of the door after school. He had invited her and Klara out for a milkshake as a thank you for helping him and telling him how to take the subway to where he needed to go. And once again like the day before, Klara and Ali talked to each other while Hanna sat next to them and mostly just stared at Ali. Every now and then she managed to respond, and Ali immediately encouraged her and told her what a beautiful voice she had. Of course, that made her blush again, but after that she had the confidence to take part in the conversation a bit more than before. But every time Ali looked at her, she stuttered. It was so embarrassing. They had given him their Facebook addresses, and ever since then Hanna had been in contact with Ali. She would never forget his first message in Messenger – "You're so beautiful!" She was absolutely ecstatic over it. From then on, he picked her up from school every afternoon and drove her home. And they would meet up alone, without Klara or anyone else around. He was always very polite, not at all pushy. And he kept telling her how pretty he thought she was. He liked everything about her: how she laughed, how she would look away embarrassedly and even how she blushed. It was a miracle, because normally boys were only interested in Klara, and she was always standing in her shadow. Ali, however, seemed to like her more. Last Saturday he had actually taken her to the nightclub with him. He knew the bouncer, so they both got in despite the fact that Hanna was well under twenty. It was a great evening. Most of the time they spent dancing in a tight embrace. And finally, they kissed. Hanna had kissed other boys before, but usually the boy, if not both of them, had been drunk and it didn't really mean anything to her. However, this kiss with Ali had been electrifying to her, the feeling had rippled through her entire body like a wave.

Yesterday he had picked her up once again, as always in his black sports car, and he had taken her to the *Mall of Scandinavia* in Solna to do some shopping for her. He bought lots of clothes for her, which she didn't want to accept at first. But he said that his girlfriend was the most beautiful girl in the mall and that everyone should see that. So, she changed and put the new clothes on right away. Black high-heeled shoes, a light blue dress, a short jacket - she instantly looked like a completely different person. She was proud to stroll through the mall beside him, holding his arm. It had been the most wonderful afternoon of her life.

And now yet another week of school was starting. What was the point of it? She only wanted to be with Ali. He seemed to have enough money, and he had said that he wanted to buy her loads of other things - for their life together. But there was at least one good thing about school - Ali would pick her up and she would be able to see him. She was looking forward to that. That thought was enough to give her the energy she needed to finally get up. She took off her pyjamas and got in the shower. As she lathered soap on herself, all she could think of was how it would feel to have his hands running over her bare skin.

***

She was sitting with Klara in the school cafeteria, they were picking at the stew. The school kitchen staff somehow managed to put too much salt in every meal.

Klara looked up; her bright eyes sparkled under her long eyelashes. "Will he pick you up again today?"

Hanna nodded.

"What does he really want from you?"

Hanna stared at her. "What do you mean?"

"Well, you know. A guy that age, with all that money, why would he have a crush on you of all people?"

Hanna blushed. "Because I'm not as pretty as you are? Is that what you mean?" she shot back. Why couldn't Klara be happy for her that she had a boyfriend?

Klara put her hand on Hanna's arm. "No, sorry."

"Well, how did you mean it then? This one time a guy has a crush on me, and already you begrudge me that? I thought you were my friend." Hanna was angry.

"Of course, I'm happy for you. Calm down now. I'm just saying, I hope he's sincere and means it."

"Do you ever wonder about that with your admirers? Or only when it comes to me?" Hanna pulled her arm away from Klara.

"My guys are nothing like Ali."

"Oh, so now he's the problem. At first you thought he was great too." Hanna got up and grabbed her smartphone. She turned around and headed for the exit. She just left her food on the table. It hadn't tasted good anyway, Klara could go ahead and clear the table.

"Hanna, I didn't mean it like that. Come on now, don't get so offended," Klara shouted after her.

But Hanna didn't turn around, she just wanted to get out of there. She passed a table where several of her classmates were sitting and they were looking towards her. They would have something to gossip about now, but she didn't care about that either.

She ran out of the cafeteria, went a little way down the hall and entered the library. There she sat down at a table, all alone in a corner. Damn, now Klara started in with her about it too. Her mother, the dumb bitch, had barked up the same tree. "He is much too old for you, who knows what he really wants from you. Probably just wants to get you in the sack once and then off he goes." Hanna regretted even telling her about Ali. But her mother had asked her where she got the new clothes from, and that's when she told her about him. A boy was finally interested in her and immediately everyone got on her case and drove her crazy about it. Why did the few years age difference matter? She thought it was great that Ali was older, because he was so self-confident and that made her stronger as well. Finally.

At least her mother had promised not to say anything to her father, otherwise there would probably have been quite a commotion. If he flipped out, it could mean a good beating.

2

Two weeks later, the time had come. Ali took her back to his apartment, which was only a stone's throw away from her school, and she could walk there from the subway station in about ten minutes. How convenient!

Ali made coffee, a mocha in a small metal jar. He also served her favorite snack: rice cakes with dark chocolate. It was so sweet of him to remember that. Ali also put on some music – Wiktoria, who Hanna loved to listen to.

After drinking their coffee, he took her in his arms and caressed her. Then they kissed intensively for a long time. Hanna grew hot, and a wave of sensations raged through her body. His hand wandered under her shirt, she got goose bumps and held very still. This was what she had wanted for so long.

"Are you all right?" He looked at her with his dark eyes.

Hanna nodded. She couldn't get a single word out, because she was so nervous.

"Are you sure that you want to do this?"

She nodded again.

"We can wait some more ...," he whispered to her.

She shook her head vehemently. But she was happy that he was so considerate and had asked her twice.

Ali started to undress her slowly, stroking and kissing her again and again. Hanna sensed how her thighs became increasingly sensitive and how she became wet in between them. Ali quickly took off his clothes too; Hanna was unable to help him; her hands were shaking too much. Once more he looked at her questioningly and when she once again nodded determinedly, he finally penetrated her. It only hurt for a moment, then she felt him inside her. It was wonderful, even more so than she had imagined it would be. He was moving in and out of her and she couldn't stop it, the climax came quickly, and it hit her like an earthquake. It was much, much better than when she did it to herself. Ali moaned too - he came shortly after her. They were both sweating, their bodies were sticking together. She lay in his arms for a long time afterwards, she had never felt so good.

***

That evening, after she had gone to bed and turned off the lights, she thought back to the big event. Yes, they did it! Hanna was so happy.

Only now were they a real couple. Ali talked a lot about wanting a life together with her and as soon as possible. At first, she thought everything was moving too fast, but now she was ready for it. She loved Ali more than anything. She didn't want to live with her parents anymore, and she was sick of school anyway. All that mattered was being with Ali. He called her "princess", she liked that a lot. And he treated her like one. He could read every wish from her eyes. She only had to look into a shop window to admire something on display, and he ran in and bought it for her - money didn't seem to matter.

Her greatest wish was to live with Ali in his apartment in Tulegatan. Away from her father, who was constantly bellowing and who was not afraid to slap her. Away from her stupid sister, who was always annoying and could never keep quiet. Away from her mother, who nagged her nonstop. No, she wouldn't miss any of them. And Ali would take good care of her, she knew that.

She didn't care about school. Everything was absolutely boring. She had hardly any contact to the others in her class, the only friend she had was Klara. She would definitely keep in touch with her. They had made up, although Hanna was now more careful with what she said to her. In time, Klara would see for herself that the relationship with Ali was serious. And then there would be no more arguments about it. In any case, Klara always had a boyfriend anyhow. She was never lacking for any nice boys with whom she went out for a few weeks, mostly guys from her school. At some point she would also find the right one, and then the four of them could do things together. That would be nice.

June 2018

3

lin waited outside the house in Valhallavägen. She didn't really think that the woman she was supposed to be watching would come out again today, but she would have to wait a while longer. The woman's employer assumed that his employee wanted to hand over confidential data to a competitor. At least the lady had taken some documents out of the office today – so it was possible that she would meet someone else. The GPS tracker was already mounted on her Saab. If she drove anywhere, Elin would be ready. She had the iPad lying next to her on the seat, the dot flashing red on the map. She looked at the clock, it was just after six, it could end up being a long evening. At least she had found a good parking space, she had a clear view of the house door and could watch it without having to twist her neck. However, it was raining, which reduced the visibility a little bit. All the more likely that the lady would take her car.

She didn't particularly like these surveillance jobs, mostly because they were dreadfully boring. She had originally imagined that working as a private detective would be much more exciting. She and her colleague Lars, however, had also worked on several exciting assignments, and she had learned two things: First, these cases could be extremely dangerous. Even though this generally did not worry Elin that much, she certainly did not want to have to deal with violent situations on a daily basis either. Second, she had to accept that there weren't always going to be a lot of exciting cases to work on when making a living as a private detective. It was necessary to work a lot of boring routine jobs as well, in order to land the occasional really interesting story. And it was worth the wait. Only then did she feel challenged, both mentally and physically. Even if these jobs had consequences that she couldn't just dismiss - she had actually killed a man. This haunted her, sometimes in her dreams, often in her thoughts. It had been self-defense, and the bastard already had quite a lot to answer for prior to that, so rationally she didn't have to blame herself, but it still wasn't a pleasant feeling being responsible for his death. Nevertheless, this was still her dream job. She did not want to do anything else. The boring periods had the advantage that she could have a relatively well-regulated private life. This allowed her to spend a lot of time with Maja, her life partner. Maja worked as a judo and karate teacher and had training sessions almost every evening, so that the evening assignments - like the one today - did not bother Elin much.

Her cell phone rang, a landline number from Stockholm that she did not recognize.

"Yeah, Elin Bohlander."

"Good evening. My name is Göran Bergstrand. I got your number from Helena Ron. You did a job for her two years ago."

"Yeah, I remember." Elin would never forget this job, she had almost lost her life. Helena had suspected her life partner of cheating on her and had asked Elin to tail him. It later turned out that the man belonged to a group of child molesters who then abducted a little girl. When Elin tried to free her, she herself became a prisoner. But this was a closed case - what did this guy want from her now?

"Are you still working as a private detective? Well, we need help. We have a job for you."

"Yes, that's right. However, I am now employed by Secure Assist. But I can draft an appropriate contract. What is it about?" She had accepted Helena's job privately at that time and she wouldn't do that again, but maybe there was a commission in it for her if she landed a new job - Lars had an agreement with the boss.

"Our daughter Hanna has disappeared."

"Oh, I see. Now you're worried. How old is she?"

"She just turned sixteen. She's been gone for a week."

"What happened? Do you think she was kidnapped? Or did she choose to disappear of her own volition?"

"Oh, yeah, that's ... It looks like she just ran off."

In other words, a runaway, Elin thought. What reason could she have had? "Have you gone to the police?"

"Yes, we reported her missing. But they just put her on a list, and that was it. That's all they do."

"We know all about that. Yes, we have searched for and found several missing people. I'll talk to my boss and draw up a contract. Then I could drop by tomorrow morning. Would that be okay?"

"Um, we work during the day. Later in the afternoon would be better."

"Okay, 5 PM?"

"Good."

Elin explained the terms of the contract to him, Göran seemed to swallow hard at the daily rate. Then she asked him to send her his name and address in a text message.

Elin hung up. That sounded so exciting. You could see how a recommendation paid off. She thought of Helena. How was she doing? After the trial against her boyfriend, she had struggled quite a bit, she had not suspected anything of the crimes and had been completely blindsided. Hopefully Helena had pulled herself together again. In any case, it was nice of her to recommend Elin. Should Elin get in touch with her to say thank you and to hear how things are going with her? She would think about it, maybe see what Maja thought.

Concerning the assignment, she had to speak to Lars first if she wanted to have any chance of getting the commission money. She would call him about it right away. When he wasn't away on business, he was probably sitting at home. He had been divorced for a while and had moved into an apartment in Solna.

He picked up right away.

"Hi, Lars. I just got an interesting call. A young girl is missing, and they want us to look for her."

"Oh okay, and why are they calling you?"

"They got my number from Helena, you know, the one from the child molester job."

"How could I forget that one..."

"I know. Listen, I thought you made a deal with Tobias that we could get a commission, right?"

"Yes, that's right. It's been a while, though, and I haven't made use of it yet. But you're right, if we bring in the job, Tobias should pay for it. But then it has to go through me, because that agreement doesn't apply to you. I'll pay you the full net amount."

"Sounds good, we can share."

"We'll talk about that later. I'll discuss it with Tobias."

"Are you in on it, then? We're supposed to meet with her parents tomorrow at 5 PM."

"Yeah, that works. I have to reschedule an appointment, but I'll manage."

"Okay, see you tomorrow then."

After hanging up, Elin saw that she had received a message. It was the address of the Bergstrands, including phone numbers and door code. Elin started thinking. So, the girl's name was Hanna Bergstrand and she was sixteen years old. You would certainly find some information about her online. Elin opened her Facebook app and searched her name, but unfortunately there were many Hanna Bergstrands in Sweden. However, when she narrowed the search down to Stockholm, only a handful were left. Of those, only one was a teenager, so that had to be her. She would have her parents confirm that tomorrow. Hanna's profile picture showed a young girl with light hair and gray eyes. It appeared to have been taken in front of her school. She was wearing a lot of make-up and smiled into the camera, but she still wasn't all that pretty, Elin thought. There was a post about dancing with her friend Klara. Apart from that, the profile seemed quite inactive. The '*About*' tab didn't yield much either: single, living in Sundbyberg. There was nothing to be found under the '*Friends* ' tab, most likely the majority of the profile was set to 'private', so that either only her friends or even nobody but herself could view it. Unusual for a young girl, but not surprising for someone who ran away and didn't want to be found.

Elin grinned, definitely something else than routine surveillance.

.

4

Lars put away his coffee cup. The kitchen was small but functional. He didn't have to do much in this room in regard to furnishing it, because the built-in kitchen cabinets and all the appliances were in perfect condition. But the rest of the apartment remained more or less unfinished. Up to now, he lacked the drive to take care of the furnishings. There were boxes everywhere still waiting to be unpacked.

He sighed. That had not been his plan, but Lisa had not backed down. Every time a job became dangerous, she got upset. A year and a half ago she'd threatened him with divorce if he didn't find another solution. In other words, a job that didn't involve dangerous situations. He had deliberated back and forth for a long time but had not been able to bring himself to do anything else. If he were to be completely honest, it was precisely those thrilling moments in this job that he particularly enjoyed. He had negotiated a hiatus period with Lisa, after which they would talk. But it never came to that. Instead, he was assigned a job he couldn't get out of and which ultimately saved the lives of two women. But once again he ended up in the hospital. It wasn't even anything really bad. Just a few broken ribs and several bruises that healed in a few weeks. Lisa didn't make a scene at first and she even came to Jönköping with their two daughters to bring him home. But as soon as he had recovered, she made it clear to him that it was over between the two of them. She wanted them to separate, without any further discussion. He struggled for a while and kept trying to talk to her, but nothing could be done. She filed for divorce in March of last year, and Lars first moved into the guest room and then eventually into a rented apartment. Only now, more than a year later, he had at last found a condo that he liked and could afford. The whole process was not easy for him. He didn't want to leave, especially not his two daughters, but actually not Lisa either. However, she had become so cold towards him that he could no longer tolerate the situation at home. So, it was better to move out. The divorce was finalized at the end of last year and they had joint custody of their daughters. Of course, his daughters were not enthusiastic about the separation, but they were familiar with this kind of situation as they had several girlfriends who already experienced it. Since they still saw Lars regularly, they coped quite well after the initial struggles.

Lars, on the other hand, had still not adjusted to living alone - after fourteen years together with Lisa and over ten years with the children. Everything he did in his new home was only for himself, and that didn't motivate him very much. Albeit this was not quite the truth. He had an extra room for the two children, which he wanted to set up for them. But until now they had not come here. They had always been out and doing something. He wanted to at least have the children's room ready before they would spend the first nights with him. He made a resolution for that weekend to buy the furniture at Ikea and then assemble it.

Lars left the apartment and took the elevator downstairs. It only took him a few minutes to get to the subway, and after 20 minutes he was in his office, no matter how busy the traffic was on the streets. That's why he generally left his car parked in the garage at the office, except on weekends when he used it privately.

Tobias was already at the office, and after Lars had got himself a coffee, he stopped to see him.

"Hey, Tobias. Do you have a moment?"

Tobias was typing away on his PC, but said, "Hello Lars. Yeah, come on in. Just one second."

Lars sat down on the chair in front of the desk and waited. Next to the PC was a picture of Tobias' family. That stung Lars.

Finally, Tobias addressed him.

"What can I do for you?"

"I wanted to follow up on our conversation about the commission."

Tobias frowned. "I thought we had settled that."

"Yes, precisely. I have a job for us that's been brought to me." After giving it some thought, he decided it would be better to leave out Elin's role in it so that Tobias wouldn't have the chance to come up with any slick ideas.

"Oh, I see."

"I just wanted to let you know before it gets signed. I'll prepare the contract and clarify everything."

Tobias nodded. "Yeah, no problem. You'll get the 10% commission after payment is received. What's it about?"

"A young girl has gone missing."

Tobias grinned. "You never get enough, always these special cases." Tobias' company, Secure Assist, took on all kinds of jobs, but mainly it was monitoring employees of any kind of company. In the past, when it came to missing people or capital crimes, the cases were always handled by Lars with the help of Elin.

Which is why Tobias immediately asked, "Are you working on this with Elin?"

Lars nodded in agreement. "Correct. I hope that's okay. As far as I know, she doesn't have anything else that's urgent."

"No, I can give the embezzlement investigation to someone else, if she can't do it at the same time."

"Great."

Lars got up and went to his office. He wanted to complete the contract quickly so that they could get down to business this afternoon. This would be the first case for which a commission would be earned, albeit really for Elin.

***

Lars and Elin drove together from their office to Sundbyberg. Lars searched for a parking space, then they walked towards the yellow blocks of apartment buildings. They formed an odd pair. Lars, standing at almost 6 feet three inches, was nearly two heads taller than Elin. She was not only small, but also rather petite, while Lars had quite broad shoulders. But Elin had a strong will and could be really tough when it came down to it.

Göran had sent the door code by text message, so Elin punched it in and opened the door. The Bergstrands lived on the fifth floor, but there was at least an elevator.

"Shit," said Lars. On the elevator door was a red sign stating it was "Out of service." Lars had nothing against physical activity, but a gunshot wound sustained while working as a police officer did not make it easy for him to climb the stairs up to the fifth floor. But what choice did he have?

His knee hurt, and they both wheezed a little when they reached the top floor. Elin rang the doorbell. A man opened the door. He was on the shorter side, but strong. His face was quite round, his hair had thinned considerably, but the lower part of his face was covered with stubble.

"Hello, I'm Göran. Come in. Sorry, I just got home. I haven't had time to change yet." He was wearing blue overalls that showed clear traces of dirt.

"No problem," Lars said. "Are you a craftsman?"

"Yes, I work in construction."

Göran led them into the living room. The apartment seemed small. Apart from the kitchen and the bathroom, there appeared to be only two bedrooms. Even the living room was not very spacious, there was just enough space for two sofas that were positioned in the corner. The door to the balcony was open, a pleasant breeze flowed through the room.

A somewhat chubby woman in jeans and pink sweatshirt stood up from the sofa. "This is my wife, Paula."

They shook hands, and Lars and Elin introduced themselves. Then they all sat down in the sitting area. Coffee and water were already on the table, Paula served everyone.

Lars first explained the contractual details. He noticed that the woman looked a bit anxious when he read out the prices, but Göran signed them without any objections.

Lars studied them both. "Then we can get started right away. Please tell us what happened to your daughter."

Göran cleared his throat. "There's not much to tell. Hanna went to school last Monday as usual. When we came home from work, she wasn't there. At first, we didn't think much of it, but when she didn't show up for dinner and couldn't be reached, we started to worry."

He looked at his wife and nodded in her direction.

"Yeah, we made some calls, but she wasn't anywhere. It turned out that she hadn't been to school at all. When I checked her room, I noticed that she had taken some clothes with her. One of our wheeled suitcases and her passport were gone, too."

"What time did she leave the house in the morning?" Elin asked.

"Same as always, at half past seven. School starts at eight, except for Wednesday which starts later."

"And when did you return home?"

"I got here at four, I had swapped with a colleague, otherwise I normally work until eight on Mondays. Göran got home around five."

"Did anything out of the ordinary happen, like, say, the weekend before? Was there a fight? Or did Hanna behave in any way oddly?"

Paula shook her head. Göran said: "No, it was the same as always, nothing special. Hanna had actually been home more often than usual. She had been out more on other weekends. We didn't have more arguments than usual. I mean, Hanna is 16, she's a teenager, there's always some conflict."

"What were those about?" Elin looked at him questioningly.

"Oh, just the usual stuff. The food wasn't to her liking, she didn't do her homework, and she didn't get along with her sister."

"Her sister, how old is she?" Lars had not anticipated that there would be any siblings.

"Evelina is ten. She has ADHD, so it's not always easy with the two of them."

As it turned out, there was only the one sister, and the two of them shared a room. Evelina was in her room right at that moment. Lars asked if they could then speak to Evelina alone once they were finished, and the parents had no objections.

Lars asked about Hanna's hobbies and recreational activities, her friends and routines and took notes in his little ring binder. Hanna apparently only had one friend with whom she regularly met and had not been very active in her free time, mostly she just lay on her bed and played on her smartphone.

"Was there a boyfriend?" he finally asked.

Göran shook his head. "No, absolutely not. She was too young for that."

Lars noticed that Paula was looking down. The answer surprised him as well. As far as he knew, girls of this age were quite interested in boys. He decided to drop the subject for now, chances were they would be able to learn more from the sister or girlfriend.

"What did the police do?"

The father smiled scornfully. "They put her on the missing persons list and said most girls that age show up after a few weeks at the latest."

"They didn't run a cell phone check? Or checked with the bank?" Lars was well aware of police procedures.

Paula nodded. "Yes, they did all of that. But nothing came of it. The cell phone has not been used since the day Hanna disappeared. And she hasn't used her bank account or her bank card."

It looked like Hanna didn't want to be found. Or something had happened to her – but Lars didn't want to say that out loud.

Elin leaned forward and showed the screen of her smartphone. "I found this Facebook page here. This is Hanna, isn't it?" The parents nodded. "What other social media platforms did Hanna use? Instagram, Snapchat, WhatsApp?"

The parents looked at each other, Göran shrugged his shoulders, Paula said hesitantly, "I don't know exactly, we only have Facebook. But I think she mentioned Snapchat once. Maybe Evelina knows. She already has a smartphone."

Elin stood up. "Well, I'll just go and talk to Evelina now. Okay?"

Paula nodded and went with her into the hallway. After a moment, she returned and sat back down.

Lars asked Göran, "Does Hanna have a PC?"

"Yes, from school. A laptop. It's in her room."

"Oh, so she didn't take it with her?"

"No, she left it here. She left her textbooks too."

"So, she went to school with a laptop and a school bag, came back, dropped off her school supplies and took a suitcase of clothes with her?"

Göran shrugged his shoulders. "Yeah, I guess that's what happened. She wasn't in school that day."

"None of the neighbors saw her that day either?"

Göran looked at his wife, who then said, "I asked around, but almost all of them are gone during the day. Except for the old couple on the ground floor, but they don't hear very well. They don't remember seeing Hanna either."

Lars was mulling things over. It clearly looked like Hanna had run away from home voluntarily. There must have been a reason for that.

"I want to come back to these conflicts, that teenage rebellious behavior. If we leave out last weekend, apart from that, what were the issues that caused problems?"

Göran furrowed his long forehead into a frown. "Well, she wanted an increase in her allowance. It was always about her wanting to buy brand-name clothes. Because supposedly all the girls in her class have those. But we're not loaded. For several months now she has been receiving the study grant from CSN, which is 1250 krona per month. She wanted to keep the full amount as spending money, but we have so many household expenses, we did not want to do that. We had increased her allowance from a 100 to a 150 per week. We thought that was a lot."

Lars nodded understandingly. His girls were still younger, but he knew that all teenagers who went to secondary school received this subsidy when they were sixteen years old. It was paid out by the Swedish Student Aid Office, CSN. As long as the children were under eighteen, the money went to the parents, who then decided on how it would be used.

Lars looked at Göran and Paula intently. "You can't think of any reason why Hanna disappeared?"

Paula looked away, Göran held his gaze. "No, why? She was doing fine. And where would she go? Besides, she just started her first year of high school. You don't just run away from that."

"How were things at school?"

"Well, it's not easy. Hanna has to work hard, and she's a little lazy, too. But she's keeping up. Mathematics and science are her weak subjects."

"Have there been problems with classmates or teachers? Bullying?"

"No, I can't imagine anything like that. We went to the development interviews with her mentors twice, and there was no mention of this." Paula nodded in confirmation.

Lars asked for the name of the school and also noted the names of students, teachers and mentors. He drank the rest of his coffee, then inquired about relatives or other acquaintances that Hanna might have gone to. There were grandparents and siblings of the parents, but Paula and Göran had all called them. Hanna had neither contacted them nor shown up.

Lars took down Hanna's phone number, those of the rest of the family and her friend Klara. When Elin came back, he said, "We'll talk to the friend first and ask around at school. We'll also try to locate Hanna's phone. If we find out anything or if new questions arise, we will be in touch. If you can think of anything else that could be important, please call us or send an email."

Elin asked to take Hanna's laptop with her, then they both left their business cards and said goodbye.

As they walked down the stairs, Lars gave Elin a look from the side. "Did you find out anything interesting from the sister and in the room?"

"Evelina was very talkative. She was a bit fidgety, probably because of her ADHD. I guess Hanna wasn't very understanding and was constantly complaining about it. But what was interesting, Evelina said that Hanna had changed over the last few weeks. She started paying more attention to her appearance, putting on make-up all the time and suddenly brought home a lot of brand-name clothes. Evelina asked several times if she had a boyfriend, but Hanna never answered. She wouldn't say where she got the money for all this stuff either. At any rate, she couldn't pay for it with her 600-krona allowance."

"Ahh, so maybe there is a boyfriend after all. Anyway, I found the reaction to that question a bit strange."

Elin's green eyes sparkled. "Yeah, me too. I was considering speaking to the mother alone. She seemed to know more than the father."

"Right, maybe he doesn't want Hanna to have a boyfriend, and he's closing his eyes on that. What about the room?"

"It's very small, two beds, a desk, a big closet - that's all it can hold. Hanna took all her new things with her, only the clothes she doesn't like were left behind."

"Overall, I felt that the parents weren't too worried. I mean, if my daughter disappeared just like that, I'd be a total basket case. But they were quite calm about it."

"Well, it's been a week. You might not be quite so emotional by then."

"I don't know." Lars reflected on other clients in a similar situation and could not really understand the matter-of-fact attitude of Bergstrands. "Fine, let's assume that they have pulled themselves together for us."

"Lars, at least they hired us. That's also a sign they are concerned."

"You're right. Especially since the family doesn't seem to be financially well off. I hope they can pay our bill."

Elin stroked through her short dark blond hair. "That's Tobias' problem ..."

"Not entirely. If we're going to collect the commission, the bill has to be paid first."

"Oh, right. Well, I'm keeping my fingers crossed."

They got into Lars' Volvo. He split the tasks between them as he drove off. That would keep them busy for the next two days.

5

lin was sitting at her PC in the office. She needed the geodata from Hanna's cell phone and had launched a hacker attack on Telenor's server to do so. When she started working for Secure Assist three years ago, they always had to call in an outside company for this kind of work, until they didn't want to continue providing such illegal services. At that point, Elin received a crash course from their employee Carl and learned how to do this professionally. Occasionally she called Carl even now when she got stuck. He had gone into business for himself and would now accept any kind of job, as long as the price was right. The fact that he now had to acquire customers himself had a positive impact on him. Elin remembered how disgusting it was to sit next to him on the PC. Everything had been dirty, and Carl had stunk of sweat and snus, the Swedish oral tobacco. The last time Elin had met him, on the other hand, he had been clean and fresh, even though he wasn't exactly walking around in a suit and still sporting his ponytail - but that was probably beneficial for business. While the hacker program was running, Elin checked the Facebook posts of Hanna's friend Klara. Then her phone rang.

It was Hanna's mother Paula - according to the display. Interestingly enough, Elin also wanted to talk to Paula.

She answered.

"Hello, Elin. This is Paula, we met yesterday."

"Yes, of course. I'm glad you called. Did you think of anything else?"

"Um, yes, I would like to speak to you again, but alone. Would that be okay?"

Ah, this was exciting. "Sure, where shall we meet?"

"Maybe for lunch?"

"Today?"

"Yes, if that's possible. Or in the next few days..."

Elin wanted the information as soon as possible, so she would meet Paula today. They agreed to meet at the *Solna Center* at noon. Paula worked there as a saleswoman in a shoe store.

The PC beeped, and her program was now in the phone company's server. She scoured through the various folders looking for Hanna's phone number. No activity since the day she disappeared. Elin downloaded the phone records and locations for the last six months, which only took a couple of minutes. Analyzing the data would take much more time. She would do that after talking to Paula. It was already close to 11 AM, it would take her a good half hour to get to the *Solna Center*. The subway was the best option, even if she had to transfer at T-Centralen.

In the subway there was a group of high school graduates in her car, the girls in white dresses and the boys in dark suits. They all wore the traditional white caps with the name of the school on the front. Elin wondered what the high school graduates were doing in the subway. She knew that this week and next week there would be graduation ceremonies all over in the high schools. However, according to the traditional customs, the celebrations started in the morning with a champagne breakfast, then the diplomas were ceremonially handed over before classes were dismissed from school for the last time in a certain order - that was the *utsläpp*, leaving the school and the warm welcome outside by parents, friends and relatives. Elin could well remember what a great feeling it had been - finally no more school and successfully graduating. But after the *utsläpp*, the celebration was far from over. Once done, people then boarded trucks and drove slowly through the streets of Stockholm while playing loud music. There was a lot of drinking and spraying alcohol all over the place. Back in Elin's day, this had been very unregulated, while now many streets were closed to trucks with graduates and alcohol was no longer allowed, at least not to spray on passers-by. After the ride around town and the necessary shower - everyone reeked like beer corpses - there was a party at home with friends and acquaintances; it was a long day of celebration, and it marked the end of an important stage in the lives of young people, they called it *ta studenten*, which means to become a student, even if by far not all high school graduates went on to study at the university. But it probably had been different in the past, and the term had stuck. In any case, Elin couldn't figure out why the high school graduates were taking the subway at this time of day. In most cases the *utsläpp* was around noon, and before that the students were in school. Perhaps these young people still had their last day ahead of them and had only been at a rehearsal. Elin could vaguely remember that they had also rehearsed back then. The group here was in a good mood, they joked and laughed during the whole trip, even when Elin got off at the station Solna Center. The rough walls were painted with a mural of a coniferous forest and above it a red sky – Elin loved this station.

As she went up the escalator, she thought of Hanna, who had apparently run away and wanted to quit high school after just a year. What was she thinking? Nowadays, a high school diploma was expected, you could hardly get a decent job without it. Elin also couldn't imagine where Hanna might be staying and what she was doing to make a living. Someone must have helped her or was still helping her. Furthermore, there had to have been a good reason for her to have left. Maybe she couldn't stand it at home? What had happened there? She hoped that her mother would shine more light into the darkness.

They had arranged to meet in the *Offside Sports Bar*, which was located in the *Solna Center* but only accessible from the outside. So, Elin didn't have to walk through the mall, but walked from the exit of the *Tunnelbana*, as the Swedish subway is called, past the entrance to the mall and directly to the door of the sports bar, which was located under a black canopy with the bar's emblem. This restaurant had the added advantage that it was secluded and that single tables were arranged right at the window, not like in the food court of the mall, where there were lots of tables and the noise level was quite high.

Elin looked around. Sure enough, Paula was sitting there and was already waving. She was wearing more make-up than the day before. She had managed to secure a table at the very end of the row of windows.

After briefly greeting each other, they both ordered a hamburger and mineral water.

Elin looked at Paula. She seemed insecure, her eyes darted back and forth. Something seemed to bother her.

"Paula, you know that every bit of information can be important to us. What did you want to tell me?"

Paula nodded and looked down at the table. She clasped her hands together. "I... I think Hanna has a boyfriend."

"Okay. Since when?"

Paula looked up at the ceiling. "Yeah, when did it start? I think the first time I heard about it was after the Easter break, so in April."

"Did she tell you that specifically?"

Paula shook her head. "No, she had come home with a whole bunch of brand-name clothes, and I kept asking where they came from. After I promised not to tell her father, she told me."

"Does that mean Göran still doesn't know about it?"

Paula looked away. "Yeah, he doesn't know anything."

"Why not? I mean, I get that he doesn't think Hanna should have a boyfriend. But now that she's missing and you're looking for her..."

"Göran is very conservative in that respect. And yeah, he can sometimes lash out with his hand when he's angry..."

Ah, so that was the problem. Hanna was afraid of her father. But she would save this question for the end, she first had to know more about the boyfriend.

"I understand. And who is Hanna's boyfriend?"

"I'm afraid I don't know."

"What?" Elin stared at her in disbelief. "She must have told you something about him."

"Well, yeah. He is already twenty and seems to be making good money. He drives a big car and has showered Hanna with gifts. I didn't like any of that, but when I criticized it, she wouldn't tell me anything else."

"What specifically was it that you did not like? The gifts?"

"Yes, I thought that was excessive. And I also think he's too old for Hanna. Young men that age have completely different interests. I would have liked her to have a boyfriend who was her age."

"Okay, do you have a name for this young man?"

Paula shook her head. "No, she didn't want to tell me that. And I actually thought the whole time that it wouldn't last. I mean, our Hanna is a lovely girl, but she's not exactly the best looking one and she looks quite young, too. It couldn't have been what he was looking for."

"Did they have sex?"

"For sure. I advised Hanna to take the pill. A baby would be the last thing we need right now."

"That means Hanna didn't have sex before this boyfriend?"

"No, I don't think so. She's never been with another boy before."

Quite unusual for a 16-year-old girl these days, Elin thought. "Have you ever seen this boyfriend?"

"No, unfortunately. He couldn't come to our house because of Göran. And Evelina wouldn't have kept quiet if she had seen anything like this."

"And he never picked her up at home?"

"Yes, often. But always with the car. I looked out the window and saw Hanna get in it."

"Good, do you have a picture of the car? Or did you write down the plate number?"

"No, unfortunately. That was stupid, wasn't it?"

"That would have been very helpful. What kind of car was it? "

"A black Audi. Pretty low."

"So, lowered. With a trunk or a station wagon?"

"It was a very sleek car, very sporty, not a station wagon."

The waiter came with the hamburgers. Elin searched the internet with her smartphone for different Audi models. She showed Paula the TT, then the A6 and the RS6. Paula said that the car was similar to the RS6, but maybe even sportier. Finally, Elin found a picture of the RS5, and Paula said that this could be it. The Audi RS5 was a popular car in the red-light district. Many criminals drove one. Of course, that didn't mean that the boyfriend was a criminal, but it was a little warning sign.

Elin then turned to her hamburger, which hopefully wasn't too hot anymore, so that she wouldn't burn her tongue on it. She hated it when something tasty would spoil meals for the next two days just because it was impossible to wait two minutes. As she usually started eating as soon as the food arrived, this had unfortunately happened to her many times before. But this one was just the right temperature, and it tasted good, too. Elin had never been to this particular sports bar before, but usually such sports restaurants had really good burgers. Paula had already started to eat before her, and they kept silent for a while as they devoured their burgers. Elin carefully wiped her fingers. That was the problem with burgers, something always dripped on her fingers. And eating them with a knife and fork was simply wrong.

"But the thing with this boyfriend went on the entire time? From April until she disappeared?"

Paula nodded. "Yes, she met with him almost every day, I think. He picked her up from school and then they went out. She spent weekends away from home too."

"And that didn't strike your husband as odd?"

"Yes, he has asked already, but Hanna has always claimed that she was out with Klara or other girls from her class. To hang out or to study. I didn't say anything. I didn't want Göran to get upset. But I don't think she did much for school. I think she's been pretty lazy these past few weeks."

Lars wanted to check around the school today, the teachers would probably have something to tell him.

"Do you know anything else about the boyfriend? What he does, where he lives?"

Paula seemed to be thinking about it, but then shrugged her shoulders. "No, she didn't want to tell me more."

"Hmm." Elin was a little surprised about Paula's nonchalance. She didn't like the boyfriend, but she had let Hanna go off with him all the time, although she knew nothing about him. Apparently, she had gambled everything that the relationship would end soon on its own. Instead, Hanna had run away.

"And now you believe she ran off with the boyfriend?"

"I'm afraid so." For the first time, Elin saw tears in Paula's eyes. Paula wiped them away with the back of her hand.

"That's why I don't have a good feeling about this. I don't even know the man."

You're a little late in figuring that out, Elin thought. She still had to ask her last question, she thought about how to phrase it. "The relationship between Hanna and Göran was obviously not the best. Could that have been a reason for her to run away?"

Paula swallowed. "Maybe. If Göran had found out about her boyfriend ... He would have forbidden her to see him anymore. Maybe she didn't want that to happen... "

Elin nodded, that made sense. She thanked Paula for the conversation and stood up.

Paula reached for Elin's jacket sleeve and looked at her intently. "Please don't tell Göran about the boyfriend. Otherwise I'll get into trouble."

"Okay, let's just keep it between us for now." Elin didn't know if this could be kept secret in the long run, but at the moment it was no problem. The good Göran didn't seem to be so easy. She wondered if Paula had also ever been beaten. She felt sorry for her.

6

S t. Martin's Gymnasium was just a short walk from the Sundbyberg subway station. Lars estimated it was about five minutes away. The subway took only a few minutes to reach Rissne, and from there it took another five minutes to walk to the Bergstrands' home. So, Hanna would be able to make the trip between her home and school in a maximum of twenty minutes.

Earlier that morning, Lars had had another scheduled appointment. The human resources department at Telia had wanted to talk to him about several employees who evidently were not doing their job to the company's satisfaction. Consequently, their working hours were to be monitored. Telia's head office was located right next to the *Mall of Scandinavia*, so it was in Solna. That was convenient, because he could drive there directly from his apartment and then go straight to Hanna's school.

After some searching, he had finally found the teachers' lounge. Now he was sitting with one of the teachers, Agneta Holmgren, in a corner at a small table. He had already been given a cup of coffee. Agneta was Hanna's mentor and, according to her parents, was the one who had the closest contact with her. She was in her mid-forties, had short dark blonde hair and large black horn-rimmed glasses on her long nose. She was inconspicuously dressed: blue chinos and a cream-colored blouse.

Agneta looked at him with curiosity through her blue-gray eyes.

"This is about Hanna Bergstrand, as I understand." She had a pleasant, serious voice.

Lars nodded. "That's right. She's been missing for a week now, and her parents have hired us to find her." He had already given her his business card, which lay beside her coffee cup. "So, of course, we'd like to know as much as possible about her. What can you tell me about Hanna?"

Agneta smiled. "Of course, I'm happy to help, I want her to be found. Yeah, so where should I start? I don't know how much information you have already."

"Practically nothing when it comes to anything that has to do with her school."

"Okay. So, Hanna chose to study textile design. Since we are a specialized secondary school, you can take the vocational baccalaureate in different disciplines. In textile design, apart from general subjects like Swedish, mathematics, English, natural sciences, social sciences, sports and religion, there are also special subjects like entrepreneurship, crafts and several subjects about fashion, design and materials. With a total of fifteen weeks of work experience, this education is very practical. This allows students to work in a boutique or for fashion companies afterwards. If you take advanced courses in Swedish and English during the last two years, you can even earn your university entrance qualification and then study just about anything."

"I see." Lars was not familiar with the different programs in high school, because he never had to deal with them before. It had been easy for him at that time, he had gone to a general high school. There were only economics, natural science and social science as electives. He had chosen the latter, and it had been a good qualification for his career in law enforcement.

"How did Hanna do?"

"Yeah, she's only been here a year. At first, I felt that she was very motivated and that at least the subjects of fashion and design really seemed to interest her. But she was generally very shy, so she didn't participate much. It wasn't easy for her to interact with her classmates either. I don't mean that she was unpopular, but she was a bit of an unassuming wallflower. Actually, her only friend is Klara. That would be Klara Grundström."

"How did it come about that the two became friends?" Lars interjected. It was obvious that Agneta was a teacher. When she spoke, her words flowed freely - that was an advantage for him, because he didn't have to push her to cut to the chase and spill all the details.

"I don't know exactly, but they don't live far from each other. They had the same route to school, and that's probably how that happened. If you sit next to someone in the train, you strike up a conversation and Hanna must not have been as reserved and shy one-on-one as she was in a group."

Lars nodded, that sounded plausible. He would also talk to Klara. "Let's get back to how she was doing in school. You said Hanna was very motivated in the beginning? Does that mean there has been a change?"

"Yes, definitely. Well, she was weak from the outset in the core subjects of math and Swedish and didn't have good grades for those in primary school either. But, as I said earlier, when it came to textile design, color and patterns, she did well from the start. I personally teach the classes on those subjects. Over the last few months, though, she has become more and more withdrawn and has done very little. Not surprisingly, her work has deteriorated correspondingly, and she has had to repeat the lessons several times. However, she has also been absent a lot lately."

"Aha," Lars observed. "You mean, prior to her disappearance?"

"Yes, every now and then she would be absent for a day, sometimes two or three days. She claimed she had migraines and menstrual cramps." Agneta shrugged her shoulders.

Lars looked at her questioningly, "That sounds as if you didn't believe her. Didn't she get an excuse from her parents for the absences?"

"Yes, she did. That can all be done online here. We use software that lets students access all of their school documents. It's quite interactive. The parents also have an account and have to sign off on absences within 48 hours. There's never been a problem with it. Anyway, these absences were consistent with her behavior in class, somewhere along the way she lost interest."

"Any idea why? Did you talk to her about it?"

"Of course, that's my job as a mentor. I talked to Hanna several times, but I got nothing out of her. We also addressed the issue in a discussion with her parents, but there were only excuses. Not that this is anything out of the ordinary, students this age often struggle with things, puberty affects them because of hormones, their personality starts to form, external influences play a big role. It often leads to problems at school."

"What about Klara?"

Agneta looked into his eyes. "Well, Hanna's parents have agreed to let me talk to you - her mother has sent me an email to that effect. However, I'm not allowed to disclose information about other students. I'm sure you understand that."

"Yeah, of course. But maybe you can just give me a rough idea. Did she have the same kind of problems as Hanna, or is Klara a model student?"

"All right, fine. Neither. There are no major problems with her and she's doing well enough. But she's not one of the best, except maybe when it comes to sports. You didn't hear it from me, okay?"

"Absolutely, thank you." Lars was grateful that the teacher was so accommodating, certainly not everyone would have been.

"When did this period of disengagement begin? Can you pinpoint that?"

"Actually, it had already started in the beginning of this year, but it really only became obvious after Easter vacation. That's when all my colleagues started talking about it."

Yeah, that made sense. That's when she had met her boyfriend. Elin had sent him a text message, which he received shortly before he arrived at the school.

"Did you know that Hanna has a boyfriend?"

"No." Agneta shook her head. "But we usually only hear about such things when it happens between students in the class. Or when students openly gossip about it. Neither of these is the case with Hanna, as far as I know."

"Yeah, it seems her boyfriend is a little older than she is and doesn't go to school anymore."

The teacher arched her eyebrows high, above the rim of her horn-rimmed glasses. "That surprises me. I would have expected that more from other girls."

"Oh, why?"

"Yeah, how can I put it? Hanna was rather unremarkable, so I find it quite astonishing that an older boy would be interested. But of course, everything is possible. Did she run off with him?"

"We don't know, but of course we're dying to talk to the boyfriend. Unfortunately, we don't know his name. Do you happen to have any idea who might be able to help us find out?"

"Actually, just Klara. If anyone knows, it's her."

Yeah, that's what Lars already suspected. "To change the subject, do you have any idea why Hanna might have left?"

Agneta raised her right eyebrow. "No, I know too little about her to tell you that. Other girls talk about their problems, but Hanna was not very forthcoming. Anyway, I can't imagine it has anything to do with school. She's having trouble in several subjects, but she can make up for that."

"Do you know if she was bullied by any of her classmates?"

"No, I don't know anything about that. You can always talk to our school psychologist, since he's the one who's responsible for such matters. Or wait a second, I'll just give him a call. I don't know if he'll be ready to provide you with any additional information."

Agneta took out her cell phone and selected one of the fast dial numbers. She was lucky enough to reach him and spoke briefly to the psychologist. "As I thought it was, Hanna never went to see him. Nothing to learn there," she said after hanging up.

"Thank you so much." All of Lars' questions had been answered. He deliberated whether he should contact Klara right now at the school or not. But maybe that wasn't such a good idea. It would probably be wiser to talk to her after school. "Maybe you can tell me how long before Hanna's class is dismissed from school today?"

"Because of Klara?" Agneta smiled. "Hang on." She checked her smartphone. "Dismissal is at 3:00 PM. There's not much going on this week, because next week summer vacation will start."

"I know. That's why I really wanted to talk to you today. Thanks again for making it possible."

"Yes, I hope it was helpful. And, of course, I hope that Hanna will show up again soon. And then return to us with renewed spirit after the vacation. She'll need some extra support after something like this."

Lars nodded and got up. After he had said goodbye, he left the building and walked to his Volvo in the parking lot. The school was in the middle of a small business park, surrounded by office buildings. He saw signs of companies like Fabege, Unilever, Webhallen and Coop. An unusual location for a school, but perhaps it wasn't a bad spot for such vocational training programs. For now, he would eat lunch somewhere and then try to catch Klara at three when school ends. He would send her a text message now.

***

Klara sat opposite him. She had texted back and suggested that they meet here in the small café *Foodwise* near the Sundbyberg Center subway station. Lars had driven straight here and had lunch. They served Lebanese dishes and there was a lot to choose from.

Klara was a completely different type than Hanna – from what he knew of her from descriptions. Whereas Hanna was clearly very shy and reserved, Klara approached him with a beaming smile and started speaking to him right off the bat. Lars had been unsure before the meeting whether Elin would not have been the better choice, as Elin was eleven years younger than him and therefore better suited both in terms of age and gender for talking to Klara. Plus, his height

53

was sometimes a disadvantage. His six feet two inches could be a bit daunting, even if he tried to make up for it with a friendly demeanor. But Klara did not seem to be bothered by his height. She herself was at least five feet seven inches tall and had a lovely, curvy figure that was not as super thin as most young girls have, and she had an engaging smile.

Of course, Klara knew what this was all about. It seemed that even the police had talked to her, so they had not been quite so idle after all. She confirmed that she was Hanna's best friend, and for her, Hanna was one of her best friends as well.

"Hanna doesn't like doing things with others. As soon as she hears that someone else is around, she shuts down. Or she might come but won't say a word. Lately, though, it's been even worse. You would get the impression that she wasn't even mentally present anymore, she was always lost in her daydreams. Everything revolved around Ali, that's why we even got into a fight."

Oh, so the boyfriend had a name after all. "Tell me about that. What happened?"

"Oh, it's nothing serious. I just didn't think Ali was a good match for her. I mean, the guy's five years older and he's always driving around in his sports car. Acting like he's a rock star. And then there's the shy Hanna. But she totally took it the wrong way, thought I was jealous. And yet I was thinking no thanks, he's nice, but he's not for me. Besides, I have plenty of other options..." She winked at Lars. "But Hanna got really upset and didn't talk to me for two days. And after that, she didn't tell me as much. She would somehow only answer with one-syllable words. She was nuts. She didn't have much time for me anymore, she was always out with Ali. He picked her up from school practically every day, and on weekends she was always busy. For the last few weeks, we only met in the morning on the train and sat together at school. And then one day she just left. She didn't say a single thing to me and hasn't been in touch since. She doesn't answer her phone or respond to messages. She's never done that before. It's not something a good friend does."

That was a lot of information at once, Lars wanted to dig further into several issues, but he didn't want to slow down her flow of speech. In any case, she had already answered his next question - whether or not Klara still had contact with Hanna.

"Can we start from the beginning again?" he finally asked. "So far, you're the only one who knows the name of Hanna's boyfriend. Ali is his first name, but do you have any more information about him? Last name, address, license plate number?"

Klara scratched her upper arm. "I ran into him twice. I mean, actually, like in person, not just from a distance. He said his name was Ali, I don't think he mentioned a last name. I don't know where he lives either, I never went there. The first time he was here in front of the school, he had a problem with his car. The second time we met him right here in this café, naturally Hanna came too. From the beginning, he was only interested in Hanna. Not that I begrudge her that, but it was kind of strange, wasn't it? He drives an Audi RS5, which he constantly boasted about. Well, okay, it is a really cool car, with leather seats and all. Oh, I just remembered something. Hanna once said that his apartment is not far from here and she could actually walk there, but that it is much nicer when he picks her up with the car. Which I understand because the other girls always looked in awe when Hanna got in the car."

"How long have they known each other?"

Klara rubbed her nose and looked up at the ceiling. "Hmm, how long ago was that? The first time, that's right, it was after Easter vacation. That's when we both saw him for the first time."

"I see." Lars was taking notes. "What does this Ali guy do for a living?"

"No idea. But he seems to have a lot of free time somehow. It can't be a normal nine to five job."

"What does he look like? You've obviously seen him a few times."

Klara played with her blonde curls with her right hand, while she held her cell phone in her left one. She looked dreamily at her coffee cup. "Oh, he's really cute. Dark hair, amber eyes, angular face, with a one-day stubble. A little taller than me, well-built, probably goes to the gym."

"You wouldn't happen to have a picture of him?" Lars pointed to her cell phone.

"Yeah, hold on. I think I took one. But you don't see him that well in it. It was when he picked Hanna up. I have to look for it. I hope I still have it. I delete most of them because of memory space, you know." Klara scrolled around on her cell phone. "Yeah, here it is." She showed him a photo. Hanna was sitting in the car, at the wheel next to her a dark-haired young man smiling into the camera.

"Please send me that," Lars asked. Klara tapped a few times on her screen, then followed the ping on Lars' cell phone. "Thank you."

"No problem," Klara said with a sweet voice.

"Can you explain why she ran away?"

"Of course, she's gone off with Ali. She got tired of school, and Ali showered her with gifts. She probably figured she could live with him. That doesn't mean she can't get in touch with me anyway, right? "She looked at him with an indignant expression.

"Was she having problems at home?"

"She wasn't happy there. There was always trouble with her sister, and her father is extremely strict. He even beat her up once. I told her to report him, but she didn't have the nerve to do it."

"I see." Lars finished his coffee and thanked her. He left his business card and asked to be allowed to contact her again if he had any further questions. Klara beamed at him with her sky-blue eyes and said yes. She seemed to have enjoyed the conversation. It was obvious that being the center of attention was something she reveled in. She was very pretty, but he wasn't sure if he liked her. In any event, he'd gotten a hell of a lot of information out of her.

7

Hanna put the cups and plates from the breakfast table into the dishwasher. She loved the kitchen. Everything in it was bright white with a black countertop and black handles. It was even fun to keep everything clean. At home this had been a tiresome task, she had never felt like it and her mother had constantly had to reprimand her, but here everything was different, it was almost like her own kitchen, she did the work for herself and Ali. Yes, Ali's buddies had been here a few times and once for dinner. There was a lot to clean up, but that was okay. Right from the start Ali had made it clear to her that the kitchen and the bathroom, including laundry, were her responsibilities and that she should make herself useful there. Hanna had agreed immediately, after all, she spent the whole day here while Ali went to work. She still hadn't quite understood what he actually did, it had something to do with restaurants and bars, that's why he was often out and about in the evening.

She cleaned the countertop and already she was done. She looked around the living room. It was so wonderfully spacious, even though the dining table was in it. The furniture was simple, but everything you needed was there. Ali had no frills lying around anywhere – no pillows, no small utensils or vases, no pictures hanging on the walls, it was a real bachelor pad. But he had said that she could decorate the apartment if she wanted to. This weekend they planned to do some shopping.

She had been at Ali's for over a week now and didn't regret it for a minute. It was just wonderful. Sure, Ali wasn't quite as attentive anymore, but he continued to call her "princess" and spoke again and again about their life together. Yesterday he said they would get married when she was eighteen. She had immediately flung her arms around his neck. She couldn't believe it. If only she were of legal age.

But Ali could also be strict. The other day, when his friend Mehmed came to visit, he had snapped at her for not greeting him nicely enough. She did not really like Mehmed – he was a bit pushy, stank of cigarettes and snus, the oral tobacco commonly used in Sweden. He always looked at her in such a strange way that it made her really uncomfortable. He had been there twice before, and the third time he wanted to hug her as a greeting, but she refused. Ali was angry and made it clear to her that Mehmed was his friend and she had to be nice to him. At first, she was surprised by his violent reaction, but then she obeyed and let Mehmed hug her. She didn't want Ali to be angry with her. And after that everything had been fine again, he had praised her and given her a pat on the ass. When Mehmed dropped by briefly yesterday, Hanna had played along nicely, and Ali had given her an approving look.

But apart from that everything was great with Ali, especially the sex. They did it almost every day, it got better and better. Hanna felt like a woman, truly grown up: a boyfriend, sex, her own apartment. If only she could show it to Klara, she would be amazed. But she knew that she had to be careful, her parents were probably looking for her and had surely talked to Klara. Hanna didn't want to have to count on Klara to keep her mouth shut. Besides, Ali had forbidden her any contact with her old life. He had said that if she really wanted to have a future together, she had to leave everything else behind her. Only once she was of age and they had married could she get in touch with her parents or friends again. And she knew he was right. She would just have to tough it out and not contact anybody for the next two years. Stay focused only on Ali. But she actually did find it hard to do. Ali had bought her a new smartphone, Hanna had a new email address and new profiles on Facebook, Instagram and Snapchat, but she had no one to communicate with there, except Ali of course. She looked at Klara's profile from time to time, many new photos had been posted there. But Hanna remained steadfast and did not contact her.

Tonight, Ali would be at home, she was looking forward to that. Maybe they would go up to the roof again, Hanna so enjoyed that. The apartment didn't have a balcony, but if you knew where the key to the roof was, you could go up there at any time. The view from up there was amazing, you were literally floating above everything else. All around you could see the small and big houses, even the nearby Sundbyberg Church. When she was up there in Ali's arms, her world was as it should be. They always took a blanket and a few pillows with them and then it was very cozy. They often smoked up there so that the apartment didn't reek of it. It was too hot during the day at this time of year, because the sun shone on the roof. But in the evening when the sun went down and a slight breeze blew, it was just great.

8

E lin was well prepared. The triangulation data from the phone company had yielded good results. As always when she needed such data, she had hacked into the corresponding server. With the laptop tucked under her arm, she entered the conference room. Lars was already sitting there with his notebook on the table in front of him. He looked up.

"*Hej*, Elin," he said.

"*Tjena*," she replied and sat down.

"How are things with you? Found anything interesting?" Lars looked expectantly from his steel blue eyes.

"Oh yes," Elin chirped. "The cell phone data gives us a good lead, I think."

"Great, let's look at that in the end. We can look at all the other stuff first." Lars picked up his notebook. "Well, there wasn't that much to get out of the school. Hanna was very reserved and shy, which didn't particularly benefit her in class either. In addition, she had clearly lost all interest in it over the last few weeks. This coincides with when she met her boyfriend, namely after Easter vacation." Lars also told Elin about the textile design program Hanna had chosen and about his conversation with Klara.

"Good," Elin said. "The mother also believes that Hanna is with her boyfriend." Elin recounted her meeting with Hanna's mother Paula. She summarized, "Unfortunately, we know too little about this boyfriend. First name Ali, probably with an Arab migrant background, he lives near the school and drives a black Audi RS5. At least we have a picture of him."

Lars nodded. "Yes, he is our best lead at the moment, but also our only lead. We have to find some way to get to him. We need his address or at least his last name."

"Right. I don't have either one. But I still have an idea of where he lives." Elin opened her laptop. "The cell phone data was quite revealing. There hasn't been any activity since the day she disappeared, and the call records before that did not show any suspicious numbers, only those of her mother and Klara. She must have communicated with this Ali through a chat app. But most interesting was her location tracking data for the weeks leading up to her disappearance. So, of course there is the unspectacular stuff - at home, at school, and several trips to various malls. But then there was one other place she visited quite often." She paused and looked at Lars. She wanted his full attention.

"Well, don't keep me in suspense." Lars leaned forward impatiently, gritting his jaws together, making his face look even more angular.

"Here." Elin turned the laptop towards Lars. "She stays in this area regularly, especially in the afternoons and weekends. It's not far from her school, about the same distance from the subway station Sundbyberg, but in a different direction. I carefully analyzed the triangulation data and it is very likely that the position is an apartment building at Tulegatan 5. It's this building here, on the corner of Tallgatan. It is unfortunately a rather big building. Hang on, I will go to Google Street View so you can see the whole building. There are ten floors. Even if a restaurant is on the first floor, there are still many apartments in it."

"I see, good. But you've probably already checked who lives there, right?" Lars frowned at her.

"Does McDonalds have hamburgers? I certainly did. In total, 41 people live there, but unfortunately none of them are named Ali. Nor, by the way, in the buildings next to it. I am certain, though, about the triangulation - this is the right house."

"Okay, so I'll assume that he lives here as a subtenant. Still, really great. If we stake out that house, we're bound to catch them sooner or later. She probably doesn't just stay in the apartment. Assuming that she lives here with that guy Ali."

"Exactly, that was my plan too."

"So, then we're in agreement. We'll start right away. Let's schedule the times."

They made a plan for the upcoming days. Elin would go there right after their conversation; Lars would take over the next day.

Elin asked Lars about other social media sites Hanna might have been active on. The parents had not been able to shed much light on that. "Did you ask Klara about other chat apps? How did she communicate with Hanna?"

"Oh, shit, I forgot about that. She talked so much that I got kind of off-track. But don't worry, I'll take care of it."

"Well, it might not matter if we can find Hanna with this Ali guy."

"I'll call Klara anyway. One other thing." Lars looked directly at her. "We should inform the Bergstrands that we are on to something. Since the father doesn't know about the boyfriend, please call the mother and tell her to start getting Göran ready for this."

Elin nodded, already aware that it was impossible to keep it under wraps for long. Earlier, she had intimated as much to Paula. Still, she wasn't looking forward to the conversation ...

She had found a good parking space on the other side of the street, from which she had a good view of the entrance to Tulegatan 5. She had been driving around a bit earlier and had been looking for a black Audi but had not found one anywhere. Ali had either parked it further away or he was out somewhere. Just as she was driving past the house again, a Volvo was pulling out of a parking space – the perfect opportunity for Elin to seize her lookout position. A stupid fly had gotten into her car and was now buzzing around her or in front of the windshield. Elin opened the window twice, but the stupid fly preferred to stay in the car. The third time it finally flew out.

Elin had attempted to reach Paula from the office but had no luck. Now she was trying again. This time Paula picked up. Elin asked if she had a couple of minutes and told her that they were on to Hanna's trail.

"That's great! Hopefully we'll have her back soon."

"But Paula, everything is pointing to Hanna staying with her boyfriend. His name is Ali, by the way. Assuming it's true and we can confirm that she's living with him, your husband will inevitably find out." Elin was waiting for a reaction. But there was only silence.

"Hello?"

"Yeah..."

Paula didn't seem to want to say anything on the matter. "Paula, you wanted to keep the news about her boyfriend between us for the time being, but as soon as we have found Hanna, we will of course bring you the joyful news. To both of you, we cannot exclude your husband. So, it would be a good idea to tell him about the boyfriend as soon as possible, otherwise it will be a surprise for him, and he might not find it all that funny. Can you do that?"

"I... I'll try to. Göran... unfortunately he's got a bad temper, I have to wait for a good moment."

"All right, do that. Good luck. But don't wait too long. We have found the apartment building where the boyfriend lives and are now just waiting for Hanna to go in or come out. That can happen today, or in the next few days at the latest."

"I understand. Thanks." She was gone. Elin wasn't sure if Paula would comply with her request, but she couldn't do anything more than asking her to do so. She sent a text message to Lars that she had spoken to Paula and that she would have a talk with Göran.

Now she had to sit and wait. Elin hoped that either Hanna or Ali would show up soon. Otherwise she would have many long, boring hours ahead of her. To be exact, until 10 PM, which is the time they had agreed upon. Maja was now in the studio teaching judo and karate, so she couldn't call her to help kill some time. Maybe she should call her parents. The relationship with her mother had suffered quite a bit since she had spoken to her parents and told them about her involvement with Maja. Her father was quite cool about it, but her mother couldn't deal with it at first, and they had no contact at all for a while. But eventually she had come to accept Elin's partnership. Even though she was still not enthusiastic about it, at least they visited each other regularly. The atmosphere was always a bit frosty when her mother and Maja met, but as long as Maja was not there, there were no problems. And so, it was a good idea to give her a ring now.

9

It was Saturday, in general not a great day for a stakeout. But the kids weren't with him this weekend, so it didn't matter at all. Elin had not had any luck yesterday, and neither Hanna nor Ali nor the Audi had shown up. All of the parking spaces in the area were taken, so Lars sat down at a table in front of the pizzeria, which was diagonally opposite the house. The pizzeria had just opened up when he arrived at 11 AM. He ordered a coffee, which he drank slowly.

As soon as he arrived, he had noticed the black Audi RS5 parked directly in front of the house at Tulegatan 5. He took a photo in which the license plate number was clearly visible and wrote a text message to *Transportstyrelsen*, the Swedish Transport Agency, and a few minutes later he had the registration data in hand. The car belonged to a Najib Abadi, aged 43, living in Södertälje. Either it was the wrong car, or dear Ali had only borrowed it. Actually, it was very unlikely that another, completely identical car was parked right in front of Ali's house, so Lars was inclined to take the second option. Nevertheless, he would wait and see if Ali showed up and drove off in the Audi before he did further research on this Najib. Besides, Elin was better at doing that.

Lars had to wait for two more hours and a pizza until something finally happened. To make up for it, it was a bullseye. Both Ali and Hanna emerged from the door, hand in hand, just a few feet away from the Audi. Lars only had a few seconds to identify them, but he was instantly positive that it was them. He had several photos of Hanna, and it had to be her, even if she was wearing a little more make-up. They only had one picture of Ali, but even that matched. The two youngsters went straight to the Audi, got in and drove off. Lars at least managed to take a few photos. He zoomed in as close as possible.

He scrolled through the photos, magnifying their faces. Yes, this was definitely Hanna. Elin's triangulation was spot on, and they had located Hanna. Now all they had to do was identify the right apartment in the house, but that shouldn't be difficult.

Lars got up and crossed the street. There was another pizzeria on the ground floor of the building. Lars was a little surprised that two were able to co-exist so close together, but he would try his luck here. The man at the counter, a middle-aged Mediterranean guy, was not very busy at the moment. The lunch rush hour was already over. Lars asked him if people living in the apartments came to eat there.

"Certainly," said the man.

Then Lars told him a story. He said he absolutely had to bring something to Hanna Bergstrand, but he didn't know her boyfriend's name. He showed the man one of the photos he had just taken.

"Oh yeah, that's Ali. He lives here. He's often in here. I don't know the girl. Probably a new flame."

"Do you know which apartment is his?"

"Nope, no idea. But I know the code." He looked at Lars questioningly and winked with his right eye. Lars understood immediately what he meant, luckily, he had some cash on him. He took out his wallet and put two 100-krona bills on the counter. The man wiped his hand on the white apron and leaned towards Lars. He looked around briefly in the restaurant and then said, "There are four digits, will the first two be enough?"

Lars cursed inwardly, but there was probably nothing to negotiate here. He looked into his wallet. He only had a one hundred and a 500-krona bill left. He put the big bill on the counter and took back the two 100-krona bills. The guy raked in the money and pulled out a beer coaster. He scribbled four numbers on it and slid it over. Lars took the coaster and looked at the man expectantly. He was disappointed. All the guy did was shrug his shoulders and smiled, "Sorry, no change."

What could he do? Put a good face on for a bad game - he had no other choice. He left the restaurant, went to the front door, and punched in the code. The door buzzed, which meant that at least the numbers were right. Inside were the mailboxes and there was also a list of tenants on each floor. Lo and behold, there was an Ali Fakhoury in one of the three apartments on the eighth floor. With that, their job was done. Hey, it had been worth working on Saturday after all.

***

The two of them looked at Lars anxiously. Paula was quite nervous; he had already noticed that when he came in. Perhaps she hadn't told her husband about Hanna's boyfriend yet? If she hadn't, this could end up being an awkward conversation. Elin had spoken to the mother and asked her to inform Göran - she had assured him of that yesterday afternoon. Anyway, that really wasn't his problem. He had merely agreed to the job of finding Hanna, and that's exactly what they had done. It was up to the parents to decide what to do with the results and how much they liked the situation with this Ali.

"Yes, I've got some good news. We found Hanna." Lars didn't want to torture them any longer. He actually would have preferred to have Elin here with him, but he hadn't been able to reach her. He had sent her a text message, so maybe she was still going to show up.

Paula shifted around on the sofa, she seemed even more nervous than before, but Göran was beaming. "Really?" he asked. "Is she okay?"

Lars nodded. "I'm assuming so. Here." He showed them the photos that he had taken earlier. "That's her, isn't it?"

"Yes, definitely. That is my Hanna," confirmed Paula. She tried to turn the phone away from Göran, but he had already seen the picture and arched his eyebrows. "Who is this guy?"

Lars looked at Paula, who looked away. So, it was as he feared. "This is her boyfriend, who she is staying with now."

Göran had noticed the look Lars gave to Paula and turned his gaze sternly towards her. "What? Boyfriend? Did you know about this? "

Paula lowered her eyes and shrugged her shoulders. "Yes, well... I suspected something like that, but I didn't think it was serious..." She became silent.

Göran stood up threateningly over her. "What?" he shouted. "And you didn't tell me? I would have taken care of that. Then we wouldn't have all these problems."

Paula had retreated to the furthermost corner of the couch and held her arm in front of her face. She was obviously afraid of being beaten.

Lars cleared his throat loud enough to be heard. Göran slowly turned to him. "Do you think that's okay? That she didn't tell me?"

"Yes, to be honest with you. After seeing your reaction just now, I can understand both Hanna and Paula to some extent." Lars stood at his full height and looked down at Göran. "I suggest you calm down first and discuss what you want to do now."

Göran stared at him angrily from below and took a step towards him. Lars continued to look him in the eye. Did he want to fight him now? This had never happened with a client before, but there was always a first time for everything. Not that Lars had any concerns about dealing with the man, who was strong and worked every day on the construction site, but Lars was considerably taller and could rely on both his close combat training as well as his reflexes.

However, Göran seemed to change his mind. He cleared his throat, then lowered his eyes, slumped his shoulders, and finally sat down.

"Much better," said Lars, who also sat down again. He decided to continue his report. "So, Elin analyzed the pings from Hanna's cell phone for the weeks leading up to her disappearance. Hanna spent a lot of time at a house on Tulegatan. Since we learned from her friend Klara that Hanna had a boyfriend who didn't live far from the school, it was a good match." He chose to leave Paula's own statement out of it. "We spent yesterday and today on the lookout there, and earlier I photographed them leaving the house. I also learned the boyfriend's name and which apartment he lives in. His name is Ali Fakhoury and he is twenty years old. Actually, he is registered in Södertälje, but he also seems to have access to this apartment at Tulegatan 5. In any case, his name is listed there in the stairwell and it is also on one of the mailboxes. The apartment is on the eighth floor, his name is on the door there. I also have the code for the front door, it's written here on the beer coaster."

Lars was trying to gauge their moods. Paula had settled down normally again and seemed to gradually become more and more relaxed. Göran looked as if he had run out of air. Lars continued. "So, we haven't talked to Hanna, because that wasn't part of our assignment. It clearly looks as if Hanna has run away to live with her boyfriend, which is why I don't think she would easily agree to come back with us, at least not until she changes her mind and doesn't want to continue to stay with him. Besides, we're strangers to her."

"And what are we going to do now?" Paula asked uncertainly.

"That's for you to decide. Maybe it would be best if you talk to her and make it clear to her that she is welcome at home any time and that there will be no problems for her afterwards. Then she might come back voluntarily, or at least you can re-establish contact with her. If, on the other hand, you force her to come back home, there is a risk that she will run away again."

"We can notify the police," Göran grimly pointed out.

"Yeah, sure you can. They can then pick her up there and bring her home, because as long as Hanna is not of age, you as her parents are the ones who decide where she lives. But as I said, you can't lock Hanna up in here, and then she might run away again shortly thereafter."

"They can arrest this guy, then she won't be able to go back to him." Göran punched his thigh with his fist.

Lars shook his head. "They can question him, but if he didn't kidnap her, and it really doesn't look like he did, then they can't charge him with anything. Hanna is sixteen, which means that according to the law she is also allowed to have sexual intercourse. I'm afraid this Ali guy won't be bothered by the police any further than that."

"Great. He can do what he wants with her and we can't enforce our rights? Great laws."

"Yes, I'm afraid I can't change that. You're welcome to talk to the police or a lawyer about it, they know better, of course, but that's how I understand it."

There was no further comment from either of them, the atmosphere had cooled down considerably, so Lars explained that in his opinion the job was now finished. He wished them good luck in their conversation with Hanna and offered his further help if they had to look for her again.

Then he rose and said goodbye to the two of them. He was glad to leave the apartment; he had a feeling that the two of them had a lot to sort out now. He only hoped that Göran wouldn't become violent. Although actually he had calmed down and remained that way in the end and would hopefully refrain from getting angry about it once again.

Now he would try one more time to get hold of Elin, he wanted to inform her how it had gone and that the job was finished.

10

li steered the Audi into the fast lane. Finally, now he could make good time. He was on his way to Södertälje, he had to show his face to his folks again. He hoped Hanna would survive the evening by herself. After all, he couldn't always babysit her. Damn, such shit. He almost had her there, she was already eating out of his hand. And then, suddenly, her parents showed up. Who could have guessed that they would hire a private detective? They weren't that fond of Hanna - at least that's what she claimed. At first, he had thought that Hanna had contacted her parents or that Klara, and that is why they showed up at his door. But Hanna had been as surprised as he had been and had even asked her parents how they had found her. Private detectives - he couldn't believe it. But at least this proved that he could count on Hanna, she had not betrayed him. That was something.

He accelerated, finally he was allowed to drive faster. The Audi sped ahead; Ali loved that feeling. For a while he had toyed with the idea of getting a TT, but he thought the interior was just too small. From the outside it looked super cool, but if you wanted to invite a few more chicks, it was simply incredibly tight. Nah, the RS5 was just right, exactly his thing.

Now he could start from scratch again with the bitch. He had spent the entire day yesterday trying to get her back on track. He'd probably lose a minimum of two weeks, if not three. Fucking shit, how much time had he already invested? And now this setback. Mehmed was already complaining about when he was finally going to let the horse run. He wanted more dough so they could have a blast. He was right, Ali had been way too patient with her. On the other hand – if he had taken the next step earlier and then the parents had shown up? No, that wouldn't have worked at all, she would probably have run for home. This way, he could get her back on the track and then slowly tighten the screws. Everything was fine.

The sweetest thing of all was that her old man had actually guaranteed Ali's success. Initially he had been very calm and had let his wife do the talking. Ali had already seen his plans going up in smoke. But then her father got angry and started screaming. And when Hanna had responded with a snotty reply, the old man had lost it and immediately socked her one. Ali had been so pleased about that; he could hardly contain himself. Hahaha. He still had to laugh now. How stupid could you be? After that, Hanna ran into the bathroom and locked herself in there. The old man had been ranting and threatening to call the police, but Hanna had stood her ground. No, she was never coming home. If the police came for her, she would run away again the next day. Ali almost jumped for joy. The old man drove her even deeper into his arms, it was just awesome.

Damn, couldn't the idiot with his shitty Ford get out of the way? There were three lanes to choose from and this fucker had to block the fast lane. Ali couldn't tailgate any closer, wasn't that idiot looking in his rear-view mirror? Finally, he changed to another lane. Ali stepped on the gas pedal.

He wasn't sure yet how to proceed. It wasn't good that the parents now knew where Hanna was. Maybe they did call the police. Sure, Hanna would certainly come back, but once the cops had been there, hell man, that was stressful. Perhaps if he took her to another apartment, it would be safer. A new cell phone and a bit of caution, then even the detective wouldn't find her. But the sensitive bitch felt so comfortable in his apartment, he might end up wasting time going somewhere else. Ah, shit, either way he was doing it, it was a risk. He had to talk to Mehmed. Although he was often too reckless, it would be good to know what he would do in his situation. After all, he'd been playing this game for a while longer.

He was up to 100 now, it felt good. Although there was a speed limit of 65, the police hardly ever came here, because the traffic was mostly too congested for them to catch anybody. Ali accelerated again and passed a Tesla, so cool.

This morning he had sex with her again, he did it with her once a day. She had to be broken in properly, he was all up for that, hehe. She wasn't particularly pretty, but she was a young girl. Her body was firm and slender, the skin was soft, unfortunately she didn't have much in the way of boobs. Anyway, with enough make-up, sexy clothes and the right lighting, she still looked very enticing. They had done this many times before; at first, she had been reluctant, but now she liked it more and more. Like he said, she was almost there. Shit, he'd get through a few more weeks. He would listen to what Mehmed had to say, but somehow another apartment seemed safer to him. He would get his little pony running there, too. When it really kicked off, he would need several places anyway. After all, it wasn't supposed to go on in his home. Yes, he breathed a sigh of relief. A little sprint at 110 mph helped him clear his mind. That's when he made the best decisions. He would send the kid a sweet text message, then she would be pacified tonight, and he could relax with his family.

Crap, a truck swerved to overtake, he had to hit the brakes. Why did they pass here? He flashed his lights, but the stupid driver in front wouldn't even notice. Either way, it didn't matter, he was almost there, and he'd made his decision.

11

Elin took a sip of her beer. She had really held back with the alcohol, but she liked this beer, Eriksson dark. She was in a good mood, not only because of the alcohol, but also because this Midsummer celebration was really enjoyable. She had accompanied Maja to visit her parents. Maja's brothers and sisters, together with their families, were also here and so there were a total of eight adults and three children. All of them sat together at a large table on the terrace overlooking the garden with a beautiful lawn and several apple trees. It was the summer house belonging to Maja's parents.

For Swedes, Midsummer is the most important festival, even more important than Christmas. They celebrate it for an entire weekend, from Friday to Sunday. Elin didn't really think it was that big of a deal anymore. She hadn't liked jumping around the maypole since she was a teenager. That's why she hadn't been there for the last few years. Usually she just enjoyed a nice meal with Maja and friends. But this year she hadn't been able to get out of it. Because of the kids, they had all gone to the village square and watched the tree being decorated and raised. After that there was music and dancing around the maypole. The songs were mostly traditional ones and tailored for the children. While this was happening, the adults drank a beer and that made the whole situation even easier for Elin to endure. Of course, there was also the usual rain shower, the midsummer weather was very unpredictable, and Swedes loved to joke about it. They all tried to enjoy the day outside, but many times had to flee to find shelter under a roof when the rain became too heavy. According to some, this is how light beer was invented – strong beer diluted with rain.

Elin got up to get another beer. The bottles were kept under shade in a large tub filled with water. Maja's brother Arvid had just opened a bottle. He had rolled up the sleeves of his blue shirt and one of the front shirttails had slipped out of his pants. Arvid had a substantial belly, he didn't seem to have the same interest in sports as his sister.

"Would you like one too?"

"I'd love it."

Arvid handed her his bottle and pulled a new one out of the water. "So, Elin. How's the detective work going?" he asked.

"At the moment, it's on hold. I'm on vacation." Elin chuckled.

"Yeah, of course, but have you had any more sensational cases?"

Elin had a good idea what Arvid was alluding to. Two of their cases had been heavily covered by the media, and their company had also been mentioned. As a result, Secure Assist had gained a good reputation and Tobias, their boss, barely managed to keep up with all the work. Still, most of the cases were just routine matters requiring boring surveillance by the detectives. However, everyone in the industry knew that Secure Assist was the company of choice when it came to handling extraordinary tasks.

"You mean like a year and a half ago when we saved those two women from that Russian perp?"

"Exactly. And then there was that case with those child molesters ... Even Maja was part of that."

Elin nodded. Maja and Lars had rescued Elin after she tried to free a little girl on her own and got captured herself. She was still in contact with little Ebba, who was doing much better now. She even returned to school, although the healing process had taken a long time and would probably never be entirely over.

"No, nothing like that has happened since then. Unfortunately, I want to add, because this is a much more exciting work than the usual cases we deal with on a daily basis."

"What else do you do?"

"Oh, mostly it's about proving that an employee is not performing their job properly. Another is about them illegally sharing business documents, for example with competitors. Sadly, all of that is rather boring. However, before my vacation, we had a slightly different case. We were supposed to find a young girl who had run away from home."

"Well, that sounds interesting. Did you find her?"

"Yes, that wasn't so difficult. We had already found her by the third day." Actually, Elin thought that it had all happened much too fast. At long last an exciting assignment and it was already solved. However, she wasn't so certain that the problems of the Bergstrands were resolved.

"That was quick. How did you do that?"

"We found out immediately that she had a boyfriend, and by tracing her phone, we located his apartment. We went there to stake out the place and my colleague was able to identify the girl."

"*Skål.*" Arvid raised his bottle. "To your success. I'm sure the parents were grateful for your work."

Elin toasted with him and took a sip; the beer was just the right temperature.

"Yes, on the one hand. At least now they know where their daughter is. But she still refuses to return home."

Paula had contacted Elin two days later and wasn't happy at all. Apparently Göran had screwed up the reunion with Hanna by not following Lars' advice and as a result Hanna became completely obstinate. While the father was still contemplating calling the police, Paula was sad that Hanna didn't want to come home and was afraid that she might seek new shelter. But at least she was able to keep in touch with Hanna. However, Göran wanted Hanna to live at home again no matter what. Elin had not been able to help her with that, because she was a detective and thus not able to repair the relationship between daughter and parents. And forcing Hanna back to her parents was not part of her job, and it was also illegal, because only the police had the authority to do so.

"Why not? Are there problems with the parents? Or is the boyfriend so great?"

"I think both. But then all of that no longer falls within our scope of responsibility. Others have to help and that is if it can be resolved at all."

"I understand. Are you satisfied with that? When you only deal with the consequences so to speak and not the causes?"

"Well, yeah. It is of course nicer if the customers are completely happy after the case has been solved. But to be honest, this is almost never the case. Even with the spectacular cases you mentioned, there were some problems afterwards. I mean injuries, for example." She didn't even want to talk about the deaths. "How about you? You work at the tax office, so you don't make people happy either, do you?"

Arvid laughed. "No, the taxman rarely brings good news. But I work in IT, I'm just responsible for the employees' software applications. And if I can solve the employees' computer problems, then of course they're satisfied. Luckily, I don't have to deal with people's tax issues."

"That works out then." Elin drank some more of her beer. Arvid cheered her and went back to the table. Elin stayed behind to ponder over everything. She hadn't really reflected on it yet, but this case with Hanna hadn't affected her as much as others. For one thing, she had never met Hanna in person, and for another, nothing bad had happened to the girl. That had been much worse in other cases, where people had been abducted against their will, and Elin had clearly felt the despair of the relatives. Indeed, Paula had been worried, but they had found the girl safe and sound two days after meeting with her. As a result, the whole thing hadn't been that tragic and Elin hadn't felt the need to follow up on it. Lars wouldn't have allowed that either, since the case was closed. On other occasions, though, Elin had nevertheless continued to dig into a case. She had been plagued by the fact that her cases had not been completely solved and then - even against Lars' orders - she had dogged her way on like a terrier. Sometimes she had burnt her fingers, but in retrospect, it had always been right not to give up. Lars had no qualms about ticking off a case when the job was done. All that mattered to him was that they had finished what they were hired to do. If there was no more money, he wouldn't even lift another finger, despite the fact that Lars had been a cop in the past and should have an interest in ensuring justice was served. However, he seemed to have lost that desire as a detective. How often had they had this discussion? Elin then always appeared as the idealistic do-gooder, even if she didn't feel that way herself. She wasn't affected all that much by the injustices she heard about in the news, because she didn't feel responsible. But when she took on a case, then she was responsible. And according to her understanding of responsibility, it was imperative that a case be brought to a satisfactory conclusion. To achieve this, she was determined to clarify the whole story and not leave loose ends. Yes, that was probably it. She wasn't a do-gooder or justice activist, but she just hated to leave things half-finished. Besides, she was much too curious to close a case without having uncovered the entire story.

Elin decided right then, next to the tub full of beer bottles, to follow up on Hanna's case. She would call Paula after her vacation and ask how things had worked out.

Maja called for her, so Elin got moving. By now, she had already half finished her beer again, in fact, she could take a second bottle with her. She went back and grabbed one.

July 2018

12

Hanna made a hamburger for dinner. Ali was out again. The new apartment was unfortunately not as nice as the one in Tulegatan. Smaller, not as comfortably furnished, and everything was worn out. There wasn't even a dishwasher in the kitchen, and the TV was tiny. The tiles in the bathroom were in an old-fashioned turquoise, some were cracked. On top of all that, the apartment was located in a huge housing block in Botkyrka, to the south of Stockholm. Here there was nothing but houses, no restaurants or shops, apart from the shopping center. But she knew why they had moved. She was lucky that Ali had been able to organize something so quickly. Because she didn't want her parents to pop up all the time and chew her ear off about returning home. There was no way she was going back, especially not to her father. She was certain that the first thing that would happen is that he would give her a good beating. Damn, he had been pissed. She was relieved when they finally left the apartment. But she didn't feel safe there anymore. What if they got the cops involved? Then she'd be back home for a while, until the next opportunity presented itself. No, it was better to be here.

Ali had been really sweet after the scene with her parents, had helped her recover, bought her wonderful things, even a gold ring with diamonds. Maybe they were zircons, she couldn't tell the difference. Ali had said they were diamonds. The ring must have cost a fortune. Hanna twisted it on her finger, it was so beautiful. She'd never had a ring like it before.

The thing she missed most in the new place were the trips they used to take to the rooftop. There was no access to the flat roof here, nor did the apartment have a balcony. She had always enjoyed sitting on the roof with Ali, looking over the houses and smoking together. Those had been such wonderful moments. But Ali had kept the apartment in Tulegatan, maybe they could go back and visit from time to time. And they could move there again when Hanna was eighteen.

The only advantage of the new apartment was that all the windows faced north. It was really hot right now, in the 90s every day. Since the sun was blazing down from the sky for eighteen hours a day at this time of year and there were almost no clouds in sight, the apartments became very hot inside. Fans and portable air conditioners were already sold out everywhere. It was also warm in her apartment, but because there was no direct sunlight, it was bearable. She looked out of the window, indeed, once again a blue sky without a single cloud. She would ask Ali if they could go swimming again tomorrow. There was a great swimming spot in Slagsta, the drive there took only five minutes. The bathing area had a sandy beach and a long wooden jetty from which you could jump into the water. You could spread out your blanket under trees on the flat rocks, make yourself comfortable and enjoy the view of the water. She loved to lie there with Ali. He looked fantastic in bathing trunks, well-trained and without an ounce of fat - all the girls looked at him longingly. Too bad she couldn't send Klara a few pictures.

It was like a vacation. Hanna was very happy; you couldn't wish for a better man than Ali. Naturally he had to go to work, unfortunately the hours were irregular, but he always made up for it. They would spend an afternoon shopping or going to the beach. And the sex with him was always great, she could hardly wait to feel him inside her again. She would jump on him as soon as he got home.

Hanna pulled the charger cord from her smartphone, she wanted to check out some clothes online. Maybe tomorrow they could take a trip to the mall and buy something nice for her. She still needed some fashionable clothes that were comfortable to wear in this heat. Maybe she could even find something in an online shop that Ali could order for her. He was so kind and almost always catered to her wishes.

13

lin was at Sandhamn with Maja. This was the outermost inhabited island in Stockholm's archipelago, behind it there were only a few small cliffs and the open sea. You could take a boat from downtown Stockholm directly to Sandhamn, it was a two-hour trip. Elin had been here before as a child, but she could scarcely remember anything about it. Only the beautiful sandy beach had remained in her memory, she had completely forgotten the charming fishing village on the other side of the island. They had booked themselves a room in the Seglarhotell, which was not exactly cheap, but it was their vacation after all. Instead of traveling, they had decided to spend their time in Stockholm, so three nights in a hotel wasn't that big of a deal.

They were having dinner on the hotel veranda. From here, you had a fantastic view over the harbor and the village. On the promenade, there was still a lot of hustle and bustle, even though the shops were already closed. But there were numerous bars and restaurants that were all quite busy. At the quay, the last ferry had just docked and was spewing out a new throng of visitors, while to the side, a large group of people were waiting to leave. The many pleasure boats moored at the docks swayed in the waves. Now, during the summer, the days were long, and the sun wouldn't set until around ten, only to reappear six hours later. At the moment there were hardly any clouds, so there were eighteen hours of sunshine a day – which, along with the record-breaking temperatures of up to 95 degrees this year, resulted in an atmosphere comparable to that found in southern countries. In Sweden, people usually looked forward to the sun, because it didn't shine that often and the winter was long. But the last few weeks had changed people's minds, now shade and a cooler temperature had become important. Here on Sandhamn there was always a slight breeze, which cooled down over the water, so it was quite tolerable. But even the water had already reached 73 degrees. Here in the outer archipelago, this was a major exception, during other summers people were happy to have a water temperature of 64 degrees. Elin was glad that her hair was so short, because it was nice and airy - Maja with her long dark hair could only stand the heat with her hair pulled back in a ponytail.

For the last two days they had walked to the sandy beach Trouville, a twenty-minute walk across the island. Fortunately, the path led through the forest, which provided them with shade. Cars were forbidden on Sandhamn, quads and mopeds were the only permitted motor vehicles, but apart from that it was possible to rent bicycles. The hotel also had some available, but Elin and Maja preferred to walk.

"Oy, the salmon is fantastic", raved Maja, who usually ate almost only vegetarian, but today she had treated herself to fish. Elin had chosen the beef steak, which she didn't regret. They never cooked anything like this at home.

She raised her glass of red wine and looked at Maja. She put her knife aside, reached for her Chardonnay and clinked their glasses together.

"Your idea to come here was a great one." Maja beamed at her, her face was a dark tan brown, the sun was already showing its impact on her skin. She looked great; Elin could hardly tear her eyes off of her girlfriend. She thought back to what they had done before breakfast. The sun had woken them up, and Maja had snuggled up to her. This had led to an intense lovemaking session - they hadn't done it that exhaustively for a long time. Vacation, sun and a large, soft bed – these were the perfect conditions.

Maja took a hearty sip. "The weather has been something else. I can't remember it ever being this warm for so long."

"Yes, global warming says hello ..." Elin grinned.

Maja put her glass down. "The newspaper said today that a single summer does not prove anything. But it gives us a taste of what summers will look like in the future."

"Well, I could easily become friends with summers like this. There's something nice about it."

"That's easy for you to say. Here in Sweden perhaps, but elsewhere it's far from funny. And there will be storms here too, and sea levels will rise everywhere. I've read that in Skåne the first homes are already at risk because they're too close to the beach and the sea is getting closer all the time now."

Elin nodded; she had also seen that article. She had more time to read the paper now that she was on vacation. And besides, it was already lying on the table just waiting to be picked up.

"We are already doing our bit. I don't even have a car. We usually eat vegetarian, and we didn't fly this year either. I think we're trying our best, don't you?"

Maja pushed one of her black curls away from her face. "Sure. I also considered swapping my clunker for an electric car. Or joining one of those carpools. Actually, we rarely need the car."

"No problem. But we don't have to decide that while we're on vacation. Let's just relax for now."

"Yeah, you're right. It's probably good for you to get away from your cases too."

Elin nodded. Yes, that was true, she had hardly ever thought about her job in the last few days. Nor were there any exciting cases to keep her occupied. The only one that came to her mind sometimes was the case with Hanna, even though it was actually closed for her. Still, she wondered what had happened to the young girl. Did she also go on vacation with this Ali? Or maybe she had returned home after all? Had something possibly gone wrong with Ali?

14

Hanna noticed immediately that something was wrong. As soon as Ali came in, he barely greeted her, his shoulders slumped down. She asked him if there was anything wrong, twice. No, no problems. Yes, he was tired, he confessed. But she knew that wasn't the whole story. He'd never looked like that before, not even when he was tired. There was more to it than that.

He hardly talked during dinner, didn't eat much, just drank one beer after the other. He didn't usually do that, at most he treated himself to one bottle. She left him alone for now.

After the third beer she sat down next to him on the couch and snuggled up to him. "Honey, you can tell me anything. Maybe I can help you."

"I don't think so," he murmured.

Hanna sat up and looked at him. "What is it then?"

Ali sighed. "Oh, princess, I don't want to drag you into this."

"But you can at least tell me. I can see that something's bothering you. I'd like to know what." She stared at him pleadingly.

He shook his head and snorted. "It's about money."

She didn't understand that. He had so much money, it had never been a problem before. "Do we have to save?"

Ali laughed disdainfully. "No, a lot of money. I owe someone a shitload and they want it back now."

"But ... that ... you didn't know that?"

"Sure. I originally had a lot more time to pay it off, but the guy needs the money now. He wants everything back and right away."

"Can't you talk to him?"

"I already have. Today was the third time. And the last time. He gave me an ultimatum. And I have to comply." He looked her squarely in the eyes. He seemed afraid; she had never seen Ali like this before. "This is a guy you don't want to mess with. He'll break every bone in my body if I don't pay him."

Hanna got scared, it sounded bad; she didn't want anything to happen to Ali. What could they do?

"Can't someone else lend you some money?"

Ali nodded. "Yes, my father will give me twenty thousand and Mehmed thirty. I've already talked to them, that's enough for the first payment. So, I bought myself some time with that. But I have to pay fifty thousand every month." He slapped his thigh with his hand. "And I don't know how the hell I'm going to pull that off."

"But you make good money?"

"Hanna, that's just enough for us. Sure, we can cut back a little, but I don't make half that in a month. And that goes towards everything else. You know, apartment, food, car..." Then he fell silent.

"How much is the total amount?"

"Five hundred thousand."

Whew, that was a lot of money. Hanna thought about it, there had to be a solution. "What if you sell the car?"

"Princess, the car's just a lease. It'll only cost me. And the contract doesn't end for another two years. Besides, I need it for my job."

She hadn't been aware of this, apparently things weren't as good as she thought they were. "What if I go to work?" She had no idea what she could do, but she wanted to help so badly.

He looked at her with a penetrating look. "You mean the supermarket? Or some kind of store? Do you know what you'll earn? Maybe fifteen thousand. Gross, you might have ten after taxes. That' s not going to cut it." He shook his head.

Hanna was desperate. Her whole life with Ali could collapse because of this, just when it had begun. This simply couldn't be true, there must be some way to solve this.

"Ali, we'll both think it over. I will do everything I can to help you."

"Really?" His dark eyes looked at her, searching.

"Of course. I do want to live with you."

"Yeah, me too, princess. That's why I'm so frustrated. This guy, he's got a solution. But, no..." He shook his head in despair. "I don't want you to do that."

So, there was something she could do, why didn't he say that right off the bat? "Ali, please let me help you. We have to stick together. What kind of suggestion is that?"

"No, this is not for you. Even if it would bring enough money. And it would only be for a few months. But I don't really want that."

What was he talking about? Was it something dangerous? "Just tell me. Is it against the law?"

He shook his head.

"Then tell me." Hanna urged him again and again, but he wouldn't say anything about it. They watched another movie on TV, Hanna asked him again, and he finally promised to tell her the next day.

"Why tomorrow? What difference does it make?"

"Princess, please. I don't want to talk about this anymore. I'll tell you tomorrow. Then you can think about it."

She was satisfied with that. One more day didn't really matter.

The weekends with his children were always great. But Lars was well aware that he would not be able to keep it up forever. Every time they came, he tried to give them something special. Staying in his little apartment for two days just didn't seem like a good option to him. That Sunday he took the two girls on a trip to Södertälje to *Tom Tit's Experiment*, a museum dedicated to science and technology, where the children had the opportunity to perform experiments themselves. Lars rode on a tandem bike with his older daughter, Stina, but in the air on a steel cable. That sounded more difficult than it was, because both the bike and the two riders were secured by additional safety cables. Nevertheless, it was several feet high and beneath them was only the narrow rope. Olivia refused to try, she was too scared. Instead, she was allowed to take a virtual journey through the human bloodstream equipped with a VR headset. She sat on a stool with the big thing in front of her eyes, completely fascinated, and kept making sounds of delight, her little hands twitching. As she was busy doing that, Stina measured her own blood pressure. They had already tested their eyes, ears and reactions; they were particularly fond of the medical section.

Lars sat down on a bench and watched all that was happening around him. There was quite a lot going on, *Tom Tits* was a popular destination for tourists and, of course, for families from Stockholm, especially on weekends. At many of the stations you had to wait in line before you could do any experiments.

He took out his smartphone - already after three o'clock, the time was flying by fast. He also had a missed call from Elin. But she was on vacation. It couldn't have been that urgent. He decided to wait until the next day to call back. First, he wanted to enjoy the day with his daughters and so there shouldn't be any distractions. Lars thought about their last case, about Hanna who had run away from home. Needless to say, the father had made mistakes, he seemed to be prone to violence, even though this was completely forbidden against children in Sweden. But children rarely reported their parents, and as long as no outsider was aware of it, there was of course no recourse. Still, he found it sad that Hanna had disappeared just like that. He imagined what it would be like if Stina, who was now eleven, would simply disappear from one day to the next. She was still too young, but in a few years, she would have her first boyfriend, then such conflicts as those with Hanna could develop. He believed that both Lisa and he would handle such a thing with more tolerance and understanding than Göran. But Hanna seemed to be so in love with this Ali that everything else was no longer important for her. Lars had no idea how he would react in such a situation. Lisa would definitely be beside herself. He could only hope that they were spared this.

He checked on his two girls. Olivia was just taking off her VR headset, she seemed delighted with the program. Another girl who had been waiting the entire time literally ripped the headset out of her hand. Olivia rushed to him.

"Dad, that was great! I was inside a human. I traveled all around."

"Fantastic. Great job. What do you want to try next?" Lars looked around for Stina, who was already visiting a new station, at a small table with a machine that had a handle which she was holding.

"I want to go there to see the babies." Olivia pointed to an area called "From Egg to Newborn" which showed models of babies in different stages of development.

"Okay," said Lars, but Olivia was already on her way anyway. Stina came up to him. "So, what was that machine?" he asked.

"Oh, you could test your hand pressure. But I wasn't that good. Dad, I'm going to see the babies too."

He watched her run over to Olivia. It was interesting that girls had such a natural interest in babies, there was not a single boy at the station. Were the children so influenced by their upbringing, or was it a predisposition after all? There was a lot of talk about gender-neutral education, but some differences remained. Maybe that was a good thing.

Lars thought about what he should do with the two girls during the three weeks of vacation this summer. The ten weeks of school breaks were a problem for many parents in Sweden. Nobody had that much time off, so grandparents had to pitch in, and kids were signed up for summer camps. Nevertheless, this often meant that the parents couldn't take all of their vacation days from work at the same time. Not that this was a problem in Lars' and Lisa's situation, Lisa didn't want to be with him anyway. That's why she went on a trip with the children in June, to Denmark. There, they had also visited Legoland. Right now, during the first half of July, the children were sometimes with Lisa's parents, sometimes at home, while he took over the weekends. That's how it all came together, and the problem was solved. In mid-July he wanted to take the two of them to Norrland where his father's cabin was, because they had always liked it there. However, Lisa had always been there as well. Without her it would be considerably more exhausting.

Here in the museum it was pleasantly cool, the building was large and well air-conditioned, the heat from outside couldn't be felt. Soon they would be driving home, the Volvo was parked in the blazing sun and would certainly be as hot as hell now. The drive home took an hour, hopefully they didn't get stuck in a traffic jam on the Essingeleden in Stockholm, that wouldn't be a pleasant way to end this wonderful day. After dinner he would drop the children off at Lisa's place again.

And tomorrow a new work week began, to his knowledge, without any special events. Lars sighed.

16

When Ali came back at noon, he finally told her. She questioningly held the pictures of the naked girls in front of his face.

"Princess, I don't know if you can handle this." Ali shrugged his shoulders.

She had already suspected it. "That's what you want me to do?"

He looked at her with his dark brown eyes. "You wanted to help. This is Dimitri's proposal. If he sees your picture on the web, I can make a monthly payment. Otherwise he'll want all of it at once."

Hanna swallowed. "Sex with other men? That... I can't do that."

Ali nodded. "I told you so." He looked at her with a distraught expression. "I also understand that. But there is no other solution. I think you better go back home to your parents." Sorrowfully he lowered his head.

What did he mean? "Why? Then don't you want me anymore?"

"Princess, I love you. You are the woman in my life. But understand this, if we don't go along with it, things are going to get dangerous. I'll have to go into hiding. And you'll have to get out of the line of fire, too. I'll tell him it's over between us, and that you're back with your mom and dad. Then he'll leave you alone. I'll tell him I've got hooked up with another girl and then I'll disappear. I don't have anyone willing to do that for me."

Hanna shook her head vehemently. "I don't want to go back to my parents." Anything but that.

Ali got up. "I know."

He went to the bathroom. Hanna stayed sitting on the couch, she felt terrible, as if the floor had been pulled out from under her feet. Everything that was important to her could simply vanish into thin air from one day to the next. Her life with Ali. His love. The sex. The kisses, the hugs. Instead, back to her parents and her stupid sister. With all the recriminations. Then back to school again. Oh no.

On top of that, she put Ali in danger. What if this Dimitri guy tracked him down? She certainly didn't want anything to happen to Ali. Hanna cupped her face with her hands and cried.

After a while Ali sat down next to her and put his arm around her shoulders.

"Don't cry, princess," he whispered.

She put her head on his shoulder and sobbed. "Why can't everything stay the way it is?"

He caressed her neck. "Yes, I wish so too."

She raised her head. "Isn't there any other solution?"

Ali shook his head sadly.

"What would I have to do exactly?" Hanna heard herself ask this question and could hardly believe that it was she who asked it.

"It's only for a few months, princess. There's a lot of money to be made."

"How many months?"

"If things go well, maybe five."

She gulped. That was many weeks and days. "And after that?"

"Then everything will go back to the way it was before. Without the debt."

"But could you still love me like you do now if I sleep with other men all the time?" Hanna looked at him desperately.

He smiled and took her face in his hands. "But of course, princess. It's not like you're cheating on me, on the contrary, you're doing it for me. I will be eternally grateful to you."

Hanna swallowed; she had never considered it that way before. Could she do such a thing?

"But... I don't know. Do these men even want me? I'm not as pretty as these girls here are."

Ali laughed. "You just don't know it. You're beautiful, I keep telling you that. The guys are gonna be knocking down your door."

Hanna laughed too. That felt good. Ali reached for the whisky bottle that was standing on the floor, he had also put glasses on the table. He poured it and handed her a glass.

"Take a sip. It'll do you good. You can still think about it, we'll just enjoy ourselves today. Should we go shopping?"

"Oh, yeah." Hanna was beaming. She wanted to enjoy the afternoon with him.

They toasted and drank, the stuff burnt in her throat.

"But, princess." He looked at her seriously. "I have to know by tomorrow."

"So soon?" She had been hoping there'd be another delay.

"Yeah, he's not giving me a choice. You have to start by the weekend. Or go back to your parents." He nudged her. "And we've got a little bit of prep work to do to get that going. We'll do everything together, and I won't leave you alone with these guys, I'll always be around. Okay?"

Hanna nodded. What could she do? Actually, she had no choice. Somehow, she'd already made up her mind. In favor of Ali, against her parents.

***

Hanna's heart was pounding. She could only hope that the guy was nice. For the umpteenth time she wondered if she was doing the right thing. And she gave herself the same answer again and again. Yes, she was doing it for Ali and for her life with him. There was no other way.

Ali had been so kind to her, he had poured her a vodka and cut a line of cocaine. That would help her relax. Hanna had done coke a few times before, always together with Ali. She liked it. Still, she was anxious right now.

Ali told her to remember how it had been with Mehmed. Hanna didn't know if that would help her, because that hadn't been good. It had been meant to be some kind of preparation, but Hanna would not want to sleep with him again. He was a bit rough, but fortunately it was quick. Ali waited next door and afterwards took her in his arms and praised her. Mehmed was obviously satisfied, he left immediately afterwards. Hanna had always had the feeling that Mehmed was hot for her, but maybe he was like that with all girls. At first, she hadn't liked him, but lately it had improved, he was okay. That did not mean that she normally would have wanted to have sex with him. However, Ali thought it would be easier than with a complete stranger and she could then learn how it was done. The trick was to make sure that the customer was as horny as possible so that the actual act was then quickly over. She had definitely succeeded with Mehmed.

Ideally, Hanna would serve up to three johns a day. Half an hour cost 1,500 krona, an hour 2,500. This meant that they could earn over a hundred thousand crowns a month, depending on how well things went. In this way Ali's debts would be paid off after a few months, and Hanna would be able to stop. Ali took pictures of her and placed ads on several internet platforms. She received many calls, but some just wanted to chat, others tried to lower the price, and then others probably didn't dare to actually show up. But one had finally booked her, and he had to come over right away. Ali would pick him up downstairs and check him out. Even if the customers didn't like having to deal with some guy in the middle, Hanna wanted it that way. Ali was supposed to greet them and would wait in the next room while she did her thing, that gave her a sense of security. Maybe after a few weeks she would feel more confident if everything went well.

Hanna calmed down, the alcohol and the coke seemed to work. Thank goodness. She wanted to experience as little of the whole thing as possible. The condom was important, but she didn't want to notice anything else. Ali would collect the money; she wouldn't have to worry about that. And no kissing, that was guaranteed by Ali. She was only supposed to kiss him.

She heard the key being turned in the door. The door opened, the voices of Ali and someone else. And now the time had come. Hanna got up and walked into the hallway unsteadily in her high heels. A man in his thirties was standing in front of Ali, who was just closing the door. He looked at her with wide eyes.

"Oh, awesome, just like in the photo." He took a step towards her. Ali winked at her encouragingly.

Hanna tried to smile. She was wearing only red lace-trimmed panties and a light red sheer robe that was open at the front.

"You like her?"

The man nodded, he was dark blonde and had black horn-rimmed glasses.

Ali opened the door to the bedroom, where red lighting had been installed. "Go in and get undressed, she'll be right with you."

The man gave her another look and disappeared into the room.

Ali came close to her and whispered. "Princess, the time has come. He's already paid for an hour. I want him to be satisfied. Just do what you did with Mehmed. Okay?" He kissed her.

Hanna nodded. He pushed her towards the door. She swallowed and pressed the handle.

The man was already sitting on the bed and had just taken off his socks. He had a belly that hung over his genitals. Hanna perceived everything as if through a veil. The lights, the alcohol, the coke, everything was like a bad dream. Slowly she walked towards him.

The guy grabbed her thighs. "You're so beautiful..." He kissed her belly, his stubble scratched her. Hanna reluctantly put her hands on his shoulders. Already he removed her panties. After that everything happened very quickly, she hardly noticed where her robe and shoes went, and already she lay naked on the bed next to him while he pressed himself against her. It made her sick, but she pulled herself together. He stroked and kissed her body everywhere; she held still; she couldn't bring herself to do more. Eventually his hand reached her vagina and she opened her thighs automatically. She could feel that his penis was already very hard. He got on top of her. He was heavier than Ali, even heavier than Mehmed. When he penetrated her, she had to suppress a scream, and then she just let herself fade into the intoxication. She lost all sense of time, couldn't even say how long it lasted. It seemed endless and yet it was over quickly. The man moaned and was done, he rolled off her and lay down beside her. He took her hand, she let him.

Hanna felt disgusted with herself, she was sick, she wanted to take a shower. She was happy when the guy started to get dressed. He gave her another pat on the thigh, then he left.

She heard the two men talking, then the door opened and shut. At last Ali came in and took her in his arms. Hanna felt dirty, she wanted to cry, but the tears didn't come. Still, it was good that Ali was there and was caressing her.

***

That evening, Hanna took a long shower. The effects of the cocaine-alcohol mixture had diminished, and she felt dirty. After the first john early in the afternoon, two more had shown up in the evening. Ali was extremely happy with the first day and was super proud of her. Hanna didn't want to think about how she felt. With the first one, everything had been quick, and she had been pretty high, the second one had booked an hour and wanted a blowjob first, then sex. Luckily, she'd snorted another line of coke before that. The third one was an old fart, hardly any hair on his head, fat, with wrinkles and moles everywhere, she hardly wanted to touch him, but he was all done after ten minutes. But still, everything was disgusting, and she had to force herself to do it, even though she was stoned. Ali said it would only be this bad for the first week, then it would be completely normal for her. Yeah, but how could he know that? He said he'd heard it from other girls. How did he know them? He didn't answer that, just looked away in shame. She was just happy that the johns were mostly the active ones, so she could just sit back and let them do their thing.

She let the water spray over her pubic area, she had shaved all her hair off there yesterday, because Ali had said that the customers liked that. She watched the soap run down her thighs. Hanna just wanted to go to bed, she was already dreading the next day. The only good thing was that Ali had praised her so much. She finally could do something for him. It felt good to know that he needed her. She gulped and suppressed the tears.

17

While Maja was shopping, Elin made a salad with halloumi and mango, which was perfect for this hot weather. Fortunately, they had almost everything that was needed in the fridge, and she only had to wait for the tomatoes that Maja was getting. She was about to fry the grilled cheese when she heard her phone ring. Lars' name appeared on the display. She hadn't been able to reach him over the weekend, but now of all times he was calling her back.

She would have to keep an eye on the cheese while she spoke to him.

"Hello, you're finally getting in touch," Elin said.

"Yes, sorry, was out with the kids yesterday. And besides - aren't you on vacation?"

"Oh, okay. Yeah, it's not really that urgent. I just thought maybe you were just hanging out at your place on the weekends and feeling bored."

"Thank you, I'm not doing too badly."

"I'm just kidding." Elin chuckled.

"No problem. Don't need to add insult to injury. So, what did you want to talk to me about? Are you bored on vacation?"

Elin laughed. "No, of course not. But Hanna's mother called me yesterday." Paula had beaten her to it; Elin had planned to get in touch with her after her vacation, but then she had received the call yesterday.

"Oh, what did she want?"

"Well, the meeting between the two young lovers and Hanna's parents hadn't gone so well, she had told me that previously, you remember?"

"Yes, that was before you went on vacation."

"Right. Now it appears that Hanna has moved on. In any case, she no longer lives in that house on Tulegatan."

"Just don't expect me to be surprised. I strongly advised the parents, especially the father, not to put pressure on their daughter. I made it clear what the risk was if he didn't adhere to that."

"Yeah, he can't seem to change his ways. Not a pleasant fellow." Elin turned the pieces of cheese over with a spatula, one side was already a nice golden yellow.

"He really isn't. If I hadn't been there, he would've smacked his wife when he found out that she hadn't told him about the boyfriend. What does she want this time? Shall we look for her again?"

"Nah, they're not quite at that point yet, or at least her husband isn't. First, she asked if we had any other idea where she could be staying. I couldn't help her with that, no other location was shown in the geodata of Hanna's cell phone, and we can't locate her new cell phone because we don't have the number. And from what I remember, Tulegatan was our only lead. But I promised her I'd ask you again. Do you have any other ideas?"

"Mm... no. Probably that Ali guy found a new place for her to stay. We could find out for sure, but then we'd need a new job order."

"I told her that, too. I guess the good Göran wants to wait some more."

"Okay, let's see him get his act together first. We'll wait till we get the order."

"Sure, I'll tell her that. Hey, I'm in the middle of cooking. I have to go check the pan now. I'll be back at the office next week."

"Then I'll be on vacation. Enjoy your week off!"

Elin hung up and turned the halloumis around once more. Shit, the ones in the middle of the pan were already a bit too dark. She quickly fished them out and put them on a plate covered with paper towels. She hoped they weren't too dark yet, otherwise she had to scrape them off or, in the worst case, throw them away. She turned the heat down and flipped the remaining ones over. Luckily, they were good, but had to be removed from the pan. After she had saved them all, she heard Maja return home. Good, they could eat right away. She certainly was hungry.

18

Today was Monday, her day off. She couldn't take the weekends off, because there was a lot of money to be made. Last weekend she had five customers on Saturday and four on Sunday. Today Ali wanted to go shopping with her, he had left early in the morning, but had promised to come back before lunch. They wanted to go to the *Kungens Kurva* mall and eat something, then stroll through the shops. He wanted to buy her new clothes, which she had literally earned.

For more than two weeks now she had been working in this business, as Ali referred to it. The first days had been the worst. Now, some days it was even possible without vodka and only with coke. Most of the johns treated her well, gave her compliments. Some wanted to talk and drink coffee first. One of them tried to kiss her, but she immediately said no. He had tried to offer her five hundred extra, but Hanna had refused. Afterwards the guy had behaved nicely, even if he was a little disappointed. Two men had actually been there twice, one of them had said that he wanted to come every week now - so she had her first regular customer. Regular customers got a discount, and the guy was actually quite nice, in his early thirties, looked quite good. He wore a wedding ring. Hanna wondered what must have gone wrong with his wife. Well, it didn't matter to her. Unfortunately, there were also unpleasant guys who stank of sweat or were unfriendly and just bossed her around. Once she had even called for Ali, then the guy had pulled himself together and had become nicer. It was good to know that Ali was always next door. He had already suggested leaving her alone with the johns now, but she had begged him to wait a little longer and he had given in.

Otherwise, she got along well with the customers. Usually it was enough if she undressed, smiled at the men and then put her hand between their legs. Then all she had to do was lie down and let it happen.

She had customers every day; sometimes only one customer, usually two or three, and on weekends there were even more. "The money is rolling in," Ali said. Soon he would be able to pay the first installment with the money she earned. They didn't have a lot of expenses: some erotic clothes for Hanna, a cell phone with a prepaid card, condoms, new towels, the ads; it wasn't really that much. This way they could put almost everything towards paying his debt. Hanna had already calculated that, if it went on like this, everything would be paid off by Christmas. That meant they could have a new start in the new year.

She was missing having someone to talk to, someone other than Ali. Klara, for instance, even though she would naturally be ashamed to tell her about her business. But it would be nice to be together with her, to listen to her way of expressing herself and to laugh with her. She kept checking Klara's Facebook page; right now she was on holiday with her parents in Spain. She envied her, her own parents had never traveled abroad with them. She hadn't heard from them at all. Not that she regretted that; well, okay, she missed her mother a little bit, but her father and

Evelina could stay out of her life. She often wondered whether her parents had given up searching or whether they just couldn't find her here in the new apartment. In any case, it was better that they had no contact. Even if she would like to talk to her mother, it would be too risky, you could not rely on her to keep it a secret. And then her father would hire private detectives again, and who knows, they might find her a second time. No, she didn't want to go through that again.

Hanna opened the drawer of her nightstand and pulled out the diamond ring. Admiringly, she held it into the light and watched in fascination as the light refracted in the stone. This ring meant so much to her. She only wore it on her days off, she didn't want the johns to see or even touch it. Like her lips, this ring was reserved for Ali. So, she had this little ritual to forget about her job. Taking a long shower, putting on fresh clothes and then putting on the ring - and then she was a different person. She was once again the Hanna who belonged only to Ali. Now he only had to come home to make the day perfect, hopefully it wouldn't take that long.

ars steered the motorboat between the cliffs. The sun was high in the sky, the water glittered. Many of the small islands were uninhabited, but on the larger ones, between rocks and pines, one or two red wooden houses popped up. Stina and Olivia sat together in the bow and looked ahead. The fishing gear was lying on the bottom of the boat – they wanted to catch their dinner. Lars knew that there was a spot a bit further out where the fish bite well. Slowly they approached, far and wide there was no other boat to be seen. Believing he had reached the right place, a passage between two small islands, he throttled the engine and dropped the small anchor. He grabbed the one rod and that was when his cell phone rang. He was about to take his smartphone out of his jacket when he realized that it wasn't his ringtone at all – Stina's phone had been ringing. He wasn't quite used to his kids having phones now, but Lisa always wanted to be able to reach them, especially when they were with him. Of course, he too could now contact them at any time directly, either by phone or text message.

"Hello mom," Stina said. After a short pause she continued, "Everything's fine. We're going fishing today, we're out in the motorboat... Yes, of course with dad... Just a moment, I'll put him on." She got up and walked carefully to the middle bench, from where she handed Lars her cell phone. The boat swayed.

"Yes?"

"You're not out on the water in that little boat, are you?"

"Good afternoon to you too, Lisa."

"Yeah, hello. Well?" She sounded annoyed.

"Yes, we rode out a bit. Why?"

"It's far too dangerous. The little thing capsizes so easily."

For some reason, Lisa became more and more anxious. Pretty soon, you wouldn't be allowed to do anything without her freaking out about it. "But, Lisa, you have already been on this boat. It doesn't capsize."

"Precisely, that's why I know how shaky that nutshell is. The children can fall in the water so easily."

"Even so. The water's nice and they both know how to swim."

"Still, they could hit their head when they fall off and disappear unconscious into the sea. I just hope they have their life jackets on..."

"Of course, they have their vests on, you can ask them yourself. Or I'll send you a picture." Lars waited, and when no reply came, he asked, "Was there anything else you wanted?"

"No... Okay, put Stina back on."

"*Hejdå* Lisa." Lars handed the phone back to Stina. Inwardly he shook his head, somehow Lisa couldn't carry out normal phone calls with him anymore. She was unfriendly, talked about only the most essential things and made everything out to be dangerous. As if anything serious had ever happened to the children when they were alone with him. Lars tried to be nice and talk to her about other topics, but she always blocked. Just because you got divorced, there was no reason to be hostile. Moreover, the only reason they separated was because Lisa didn't like his job, otherwise he hadn't done anything to her. He decided that he would have a talk with Lisa about it. But not on the phone and not in the presence of the children.

Stina confirmed and assure her mother that both of them were wearing life jackets and that they were tightly fastened. Then she promised to take good care and said goodbye.

Lars lifted the fishing rods and smiled encouragingly at the children. "So, my girls. Shall we catch ourselves some fish?"

Stina put her cell phone away and nodded, Olivia stood up and said, "Yes, but can we go swimming afterwards?"

"Sure, we'll head down a little further to that little sandy beach."

"Oh yay." Olivia was satisfied and took the rod with her small hands. Stina got the other one, she looked a little uncertain. Lars hoped her mother hadn't

frightened her. However, once they had caught the
first fish, she would certainly stop thinking about it.
He opened the tackle box.

20

Once again, it was Monday. Ali had not come
home last night. Hanna had gone to bed alone,
feeling frustrated. She had sent him another
text message but had not received a reply. Ali didn't
like it when she called him, it interfered with his work.
Then he hadn't been there this morning either. She
had sent another message and had eventually tried to
call him, but she only got the voicemail. What was
going on? It was her day off today and they usually did
something together. Earlier, she had reached
Mehmed, but he didn't know what was going on

either. Now it was already noon, and she was worried. Ali had never done this before. He would always at least send a message, and most of the time he'd call if he was running late.

Hanna paced up and down the living room. What could she do? Call his parents? Ali would probably be angry, because she had never met them, and he wouldn't want her to worry them. Besides, she'd have to get hold of their number first.

She thought about the apartment on Tulegatan. Was he there? If so, why hadn't he contacted her? Was he sleeping off a binge? Maybe he had too much to drink last night, although he rarely did so. Exactly, that's what it could be. He had knocked back a few glasses somewhere in Sundbyberg, it had gotten late, and so he had gone to his apartment there. Perhaps he had been feeling so miserable that he had gone to bed, the phone wasn't charged, and so she couldn't reach him. But what if he needed help? She could go over there, the key to the apartment should still be around here somewhere. Hanna started looking for it. First, she rummaged through all the drawers in the small cupboard that stood in the hallway, but it wasn't there. She didn't find anything in the living room closet either. However, she finally found the key in his nightstand. She picked it up and held it tightly in her hand. Her mind was made up. Just in case he showed up over here in the meantime, she quickly jotted down a short note for him. She would go to the Tulegatan apartment, check for him and then return. It would take a good hour. First, she had to take the subway and then the transverse line from Liljeholmen. She tried to call him one more time, but it went directly to voicemail again. After that, she sent him another text message letting him know that she was going to Tulegatan to see if he was there. If he didn't like that, then he could give her a call.

The trip went smoothly, since midday Monday was a rather quiet time, and then the connecting train came just six minutes later. She got off at Sundbyberg Center and walked the short distance to Tulegatan. Many people were still inside the pizzeria, although lunch time was almost over. She looked up at the house. Oh, how she loved living here, seeing it made her feel homesick. Right now, though, it was more important to find out what was going on with Ali. She checked her cell phone again, but nope, there was no message from him. She entered the door code and the lock buzzed. The code hadn't changed. The elevator was already downstairs waiting. She pressed the eight and the elevator started to move. She was feeling pretty queasy. Of course, she hoped that Ali was okay. Although she didn't know how he would react, because maybe he wouldn't be happy if she suddenly showed up here. It didn't matter either way, she had to know what was going on. If he didn't like it, he could've just contacted her. Of course, it was still possible that he wasn't here at all, in which case she wouldn't know what to do.

The elevator doors slid apart, she stepped outside and walked the few steps to the apartment door. She decided to ring the doorbell first. She rang three times, and she could clearly hear the bell ringing inside, but there was no response. It was hard for her to make sense of it. Either he wasn't here, or he was lying half-conscious in bed. In any case, she was already here and would definitely check it out. Hanna put the key in the lock, she only had to release the latch, because the door wasn't locked. So Ali probably was here, as he usually turned the key once when he left the apartment, but now the door was just shut. Slowly she opened the door, the hallway was dark, it smelled strange, kind of metallic. Not one sound could be heard in the apartment.

"Ali? Are you here?"

She listened, but there was just silence. She went to the bedroom; the door was open, but nobody was in there, and the bed didn't look like Ali had slept there either. Shit, maybe he wasn't here after all? Hanna slumped her shoulders in disappointment. What should she do now?

She would make herself a coffee before going back. Everything was tidy in the kitchen; it didn't look like Ali had been here the last few days. She opened the dishwasher, but it was loaded with dirty dishes. So, he had been here after all. She popped in a tab and pressed start. The machine began to hum, you could hear the water rushing in. Ali had an espresso machine here. She turned it on, chose a pod and waited for the brewed coffee to drip into her cup. She looked in the refrigerator, which was almost empty, but an opened milk carton was still there. It had already expired, but still smelled good and so Hanna added a shot to her coffee. She picked up the cup and strolled into the living room. What had happened here? There was broken glass on the floor, a chair knocked over.

She froze as she suddenly stood before Ali. In shock, the cup slipped from her hands and smashed on the floor.

PART II

August 2018

21

boring job. Once again surveillance, this time two men who run a small company together. The two had worked with General Electrics for a long time, apparently on a new development with great technological and economic potential. Suddenly, though, they had given notice, and General Electrics feared that they would pass on the findings they had gained to the competition. So, Lars now had to sit here and observe who they were meeting with. It was extremely boring. Fortunately, he took turns with his colleague Marie. She took over the mornings, he the afternoons.

Meanwhile, Elin monitored the two men's phone conversations every day. That was quite a tedious task, because they had contact to a lot of people every day. But so far, Elin had been able to check off all of the conversation partners as unremarkable. The surveillance of individuals had also yielded no results. Most days the two of them worked in their office, sometimes one of them went to talk to customers, but even those had all proved to be unsuspicious so far.

The worst thing about it was that it was simply too hot in the car, as it was over ninety degrees and the sun was blazing down mercilessly on the sheet metal. The air conditioning only ran when the engine was running, and Lars couldn't keep it on for hours. So, he had to leave the car after half an hour at the latest and check around for another lookout. This was easier said than done, because the company of the two was in the Helenelund district of Sollentuna, a suburb of Stockholm. This was convenient for them, as they only had to cross the motorway and they were already in Kista, Sweden's Silicon Valley, where almost all the major technology companies were located. After all, these were their customers. But their office was in the middle of a residential area, which made it difficult to position oneself anywhere without garnering unwanted attention, not to mention that the spot had to be somewhere cooler. At the moment, Lars had retired to the pizzeria on the corner of the main street. Although he couldn't see the house with the office from here, he could watch the street in front of it and see whether a car stopped there or one of their cars took off. It wasn't an ideal situation, as he had found out the hard way yesterday, when suddenly one of them had left for Kista and Lars had to run out from the restaurant to his car in order not to be left behind. That had been a close call. Stupid situation, but he saw no other solution. He could, of course, put a transmitter on the two cars, but that was kind of overkill for a case like that; he knew that Elin had less scruples about it, but he was a bit conservative in that respect. So now he sat here, at a table by the window, always with his eyes peeled on the street, so as not to miss anything. Except, unfortunately, nothing happened.

His phone rang. It was an unknown number, a Stockholm landline. Hopefully not another telemarketer. Tobias had appointed Lars as an authorized signatory, which was a good thing, but since then all kinds of serious and dubious companies and organizations had tried to sell him on something. It ranged from advertisements to telephone subscriptions to company cars. And then there were appeals for donations for all the good actions, but Lars couldn't authorize any of them since that was still on Tobias. Lars didn't have a budget for something like that. Recently, an organization called him and asked him if Secure Assist could equip the first graders of a school in Solna with reflective vests. Sure, it made sense, but in Lars' opinion the parents could probably still finance it themselves. Afterwards he had researched the matter for himself on the internet and learned that such a vest was available for less than fifty krona. That really wasn't an arm and a leg. His children both had such a vest, even before they started attending school. As he remembered, they had purchased the vests themselves. He prepared himself inwardly for another salesman – what would it be this time?

"Lars Olsson," he said resolutely, but not rude.

"Yes, hello. My name is Edvard Melquist. I am an attorney at Nordahl & Brunn."

That didn't say anything to him, but a lawyer probably was calling about one of their cases anyway.

"*Hej.* How can I help you?"

"I represent Hanna Bergstrand as a criminal defense attorney and got your number from her parents."

Lars was puzzled – criminal defense lawyer? Did Hanna do something wrong? If the lawyer had come forward about Göran Bergstrand, he would not have been near as shocked.

"Yes, we were working on an assignment for the Bergstrands right before summer. I suppose that's what this is about."

"Correct. We have a serious situation here and Hanna is in big trouble. I don't want to say any more on the phone, but I'd like to meet with you and your colleague, I think we can use your help."

That didn't sound good. What had happened? "Sure, we can do that. How about tomorrow morning?"

"That works out well. Nine o'clock at our office?"

They worked out the logistics, then the man said goodbye. Lars wanted to call Elin immediately, but noticed when he looked down the street that one of the cars of his surveillance targets had disappeared. Damn, that phone call must have distracted him at the exact moment when something finally happened. He got up quickly and ran to the door, he would just call Elin later.

***

Lars and Elin had met at Kungsholmen, near Elin's apartment. The law office was strategically situated there, because both the police headquarters and the district court were located on Kungsholmen. The traffic from Solna to here had been heavy, but Lars had taken this into account beforehand. Now they were sitting in a modern conference room, furnished all in dark brown and black, befitting for a law firm. Nordahl & Brunn had specialized in defense cases, so this really had to be about an indictment against Hanna. Elin couldn't fathom what little Hanna could possibly have done that was so bad. At the most, she imagined a possible suicide attempt as a result of her father's intervention. However, suicide was not punishable in Sweden. Lars had suspected a drug crime.

The receptionist, a young blond girl in a blue suit, had greeted them and ushered them into the conference room. Coffee and water were already put out on the table and available here. They both helped themselves, and Lars had just taken the first sip of his coffee when the lawyer entered the room.

"*God morgon.* I am Edvard Melquist. I'm glad you could come so quickly."

Elin and Lars also wished him a good morning and introduced themselves. The man was clean-shaven, had a bald forehead and dark framed glasses. He was slim and wore a dark gray suit with a white shirt and red striped tie. Lars estimated him to be about forty. He sat down on the other side of the square table and placed a file folder on the table in front of him.

"Perhaps we should start with the assignment you got from Hanna Bergstrand's parents before the summer."

Lars hesitated. "It's confidential. We'd have to check with the Bergstrands first."

"I've already done that." The lawyer pulled a document out of the folder and handed it to Lars. "This is a declaration of consent, signed by Göran and Paula Bergstrand, releasing you from your obligation to maintain confidentiality. I will say that I'm glad you're taking it this seriously, because not everyone in your line of work does."

The document was legitimate, so Lars could fill the lawyer in about their case. He gave a rough summary of what the assignment had involved and how they had solved it. The lawyer listened attentively, and when Lars reported on the geodata of Hanna's cell phone, he frowned.

After Lars was done, Edvard said: "I guess the cell phone data wasn't exactly obtained legally, was it?"

Lars smiled at him and replied: "Let's just say that sometimes we need to help ourselves..."

"I see. Yes, you solved that quickly and efficiently. That's why we also thought that you could get back into it and maybe make a breakthrough in this new situation."

Elin leaned forward. Lars saw that she was gradually losing patience, she now wanted to know what this was all about. He himself was also eager to find out and looked at the lawyer expectantly.

"Maybe you can finally reveal to us what the situation is. What has Hanna done?" Elin shifted around impatiently in her chair.

The lawyer leaned back in his chair and calmly replied, "Of course, I was just about to. Hanna is suspected of murder, and the prosecutor is about to file charges."

"Murder?" Elin looked at him incredulously, Lars was just as astonished, he hadn't expected that at all.

"Yes, her boyfriend, this Ali Fakhoury, the one she was with where you tracked her down before summer, was murdered, and with a knife. Hanna's fingerprints, and yes, unfortunately only hers, are on the murder weapon, and Hanna was also found with the body."

Lars and Elin looked at each other. Elin shook her head. "And what has Hanna said about it?"

"That's the big problem. Hanna doesn't talk – neither with her parents nor with me. We therefore do not know what her version is. She also did not talk to the police, which is good, because often a lawyer only becomes involved at a point after the client has already made a first statement, and this has then to be revoked. In this case, however, she is not talking to anyone at all. Of course, this is not very helpful for us either. However, her parents don't believe that Hanna murdered the young man and want us to prove her innocence. Unfortunately, the public prosecutor's office focused on Hanna as the perpetrator at an early stage, and the police therefore conducted a rather one-sided and limited investigation."

Lars still hadn't been able to believe the whole thing. "Why would she kill her boyfriend?"

"The DA has found a compelling motive. You must know that Hanna has been prostituting herself in the last few weeks and everyone assumes that this Ali forced her to do it."

"Oh, shit," cursed Elin.

"What we cannot refute," continued the lawyer, "is the prostitution itself, because there are advertisements on the internet with revealing pictures of Hanna. There is also clear evidence that Fakhoury procured the johns. He probably collected the money as well, since Hanna certainly did not have it. According to the prosecution's theory, Hanna didn't want to continue doing that or didn't want to do certain things, but Fakhoury insisted on it and Hanna saw no other way out but to kill him. At the scene of the crime, everything looks like an argument took place and so we could certainly plead manslaughter or even self-defense, but for that we would need a statement from Hanna. If we don't get it, and at the moment everything is pointing to that, then she runs a great risk of being convicted of murder. The only thing that could save her under these circumstances would be an alternative to the crime and/or motive. And that's where you come in. It is imperative that we know more about the background of this relationship. Were there really problems between them? How had she ended up in prostitution? And what exactly happened on the day of the crime? One thing is a bit strange, though, Fakhoury was killed in the apartment in Tulegatan, but the prostitution took place in another apartment in Botkyrka. They probably even lived there, because her parents claim that no one had been around in Tulegatan for quite some time."

"What's the worst that could happen to her? She's not even eighteen yet." Lars rubbed his chin.

"Four years in a closed juvenile detention center, in exceptional cases even regular prison, but I don't see that happening in this case. I don't believe that the four years would be the biggest problem for Hanna, but rather that she would be branded a convicted murderer for the rest of her life."

"I see," Lars murmured.

"And is it possible that Ali killed himself and Hanna just found him?" Elin was already looking for alternative solutions.

Edvard shook his head. "No, the knife was thrust into his chest, according to the coroner, you can't inflict that kind of an injury on yourself. Besides, his fingerprints would have to be on the knife as well. I can't think of any reason why Hanna would have wiped those off."

"How had Hanna behaved when she was found with the body?" For Lars, all this didn't really add up. He didn't know Hanna personally, but he found it difficult to believe that this shy girl would commit a murder.

"Hanna still had the knife in her hand when the police arrived. She had apparently screamed loudly for help, whereupon one of the neighbors called the police and also requested an ambulance. But the paramedics hadn't been able to do anything for Fakhoury, because by the time they had arrived, he was already dead. The policemen report that Hanna was crying, but otherwise she stood there frozen and didn't say a word. The district attorney prosecuting interprets this as meaning that Hanna regretted her action immediately afterwards, hence the call for help, but unfortunately realized too late what she had done.

"Where is Hanna now?" asked Lars.

"She is in custody and is currently being held right around the corner at the Kronoberg Correctional Institution. Since she had unfortunately been unable to make a statement since her arrest, the district judge has ordered her to be detained, fortunately without restrictions. So, she is allowed to have contact with the outside world. Anything else would also be very unusual for a sixteen-year-old. That means she gets to see her family every day. Me too, of course, but it's no use."

"Does she talk to her parents or has she been refusing to say anything at all?"

"Well, she doesn't talk much, however, you can have a chat with her. But as soon as you mention the crime or even talk about her life with this Fakhoury, she becomes stubborn and refuses to say anything else."

"May we visit her?" Elin asked. Lars thought it was a good idea. He imagined that Elin could easily establish a connection to Hanna.

"I'll put in a request for that, I think." Edvard made a note. "But I'm not getting my hopes up too high that you can do more than her parents. Still, it's worth a try. Provided you accept the case." He looked searchingly at Lars.

He nodded. "Yes, let's do that. All you have to do is sign the contract, I've already prepared it accordingly."

Lars took out two copies of their standard contract, which he had already signed, and handed them to Edvard. Edvard looked at the document briefly and said that they would fill it in and sign it today. A courier would bring one copy to Secure Assist, along with the existing documentation on the case. He wanted Lars and Elin to start as soon as possible.

"How is that actually paid for?" Lars asked. "I had the impression that the Bergstrands had a hard time raising the money even on our first assignment. And this time there will certainly be higher costs. Besides, you don't exactly strike me as being a public defender. Am I right?"

Edvard smiled and nodded. "Good observation. Yeah, that's right, the Bergstrands couldn't afford it. Fortunately, there is a fund for such cases. A wealthy industrialist set it up after his daughter, who was also a minor, was on trial and almost sentenced. It was only through the involvement of a lawyer that she was released. Now there is an opportunity to apply for money from this fund, and we have done so. That's the only reason I'm representing Hanna, and that's the only reason I can hire you."

"I see. Thanks for explaining."

Lars and Elin said goodbye and left the office.

On the way out, both were absorbed in thought. Arriving down the street, Elin finally turned to Lars. "What a story. I never expected anything like this. I still can't believe it."

Lars nodded. "Me neither. And I guess this time it's going to be a lot harder to find out anything here. We won't be checking this off in three days."

"It doesn't bother me. As long as we can help Hanna."

"Well, we'll figure something out."

"Anyway, it should be exciting."

Lars could see that Elin was looking forward to the new job, he knew how much she loved such challenges. Well, he himself was also happy to be able to hand over the boring surveillance to others. He only had to clarify this with Tobias, as well as his commission for this case – it would certainly be higher than last time.

22

The sushi was delicious. Maja had brought it from a place near her studio. Having had a falling out with the director of the previous studio a year and a half ago she had been forced to find a new one. This had taken a few months, during which Elin had to take on the responsibility of paying the expenses for both of them. Maja had not liked that at all, and she had insisted on paying back everything. Now she had been working in a studio on Söder for a good year and she really liked it. Fortunately, she had managed to take most of her clients with her, and the colleagues in the studio seemed very nice. The studio also had the advantage that there were lots of restaurants on the same street, so Maja often brought dinner with her, or Elin picked her up and they sat down in a cozy restaurant to eat. Considering how hot it was that day, the sushi was a really good choice since it was nice and cool.

"I'm glad the studio has air conditioning. Otherwise we would probably have to stop the training. There are fewer people coming than usual anyway." Maja took a sip of beer.

"Did the old studio actually have air conditioning?"

"No, it didn't. However, it was on the lowest floor and facing north, so it was never too hot. On the other hand, I can't remember a summer like this either. So hot for so long, it's never been like this before."

"In the newspaper they write that it is probably the warmest summer since they started recording temperatures."

"Yeah, everybody's talking about it, global warming and all that. In any case, the new studio is right under the blazing sun, with lots of glass surfaces, remember?"

"Yes, but when I was there, it was dark, last year in autumn, and so I didn't notice that." Elin had once been there to be shown around by Maja. Otherwise, she went to a studio near the office – in spite of once having met Maja as her judo teacher. But since they were together, Elin preferred to train in another group. Not that she couldn't learn anything more from Maja, but the mood had become somehow strange when the others realized that the two were a couple.

"I can tell you, it's so bright now, we don't even need the lamps. Although we keep the curtains closed. I can only hope the air conditioning doesn't break down at some point."

"What do the colleagues have to say? Have they ever had any problems with it?"

Maja shook her head. "No, but as I said, we've never had a summer like this before, the unit has to work much harder than normal in this constant heat. People are already sweating when they arrive." Maja laughed. "We can almost just skip the warm-up; we can just start right in with the exercises."

"At least that's one advantage." Elin chuckled.

Maja took a vegetarian California roll. "How was your day?"

"You won't believe it. We have a new case, something very unusual. I told you about Lars' call yesterday. So, this morning we went to this lawyer's office and can you believe that this Hanna is suspected of murder?"

Maja opened her eyes. "What? Tell me."

Elin reported in detail about the meeting with Edvard, while they slowly but surely consumed the sushi.

"How old was this Hanna's boyfriend again?"

"He would have been twenty-one in October. Why?"

Maja licked off her index finger. "Yeah, it kind of all sounds like a loverboy to me."

What did Maja mean by that? Probably not your average boyfriend. "That doesn't mean anything to me. Is that a term for a particular kind of relationship?"

"Oh yes", Maja nodded. "Quite typical is a certain age difference, both mostly still teenagers, the girl of course younger and quite inexperienced. The older boy hits on the younger girl and first it's like a great love affair, then the girl is sent out on the streets to make money. Alienation often occurs with the parents. Pretty accurate, isn't it?"

Elin was amazed. "Indeed, it is. So, this is a common occurrence. How do you know that?"

"I read a newspaper article about it a while back. The phenomenon appears to already exist in many countries, and it has been a new development in Sweden for some years. The police have great difficulty with this, the girls are often still really young, I think it starts at fourteen years of age. And since everything is voluntary, it's hard to prove anything and pin it on these guys."

"Incredible what goes on. So, you're saying this Ali guy planned this from the start?"

"Wouldn't surprise me in the least. You should go and find out what happened to his former girlfriend."

"It's called loverboy, you say?" Elin looked at Maja. She nodded. "I'll have to google that right away. That really puts the whole story in a different light."

Elin scooped her last Sushi up that was in the bowl. She could hardly stay seated in her chair, she absolutely wanted to dig more into this topic. Was Lars aware of this term?

After cleaning up, Elin opened her laptop and went looking on the internet for information. After narrowing down her search accordingly, she found numerous articles about loverboys, both in Sweden and internationally. She found articles from England, USA, Germany and France. Apparently, this method had been in use for many years, and in Sweden the phenomenon had been noticed by the police on a larger scale since 2013. Elin was astonished that the descriptions of the cases were almost all identical, even across the different national borders. It was always young men, often even under twenty, who approached underage girls with an uncanny sense of who to target - they picked up the girls who were hungry for recognition and socially unstable. They showered them with compliments and gifts, went out with them. They played the great love for them and did everything to isolate the girl from everyone else. It often lasted only a few weeks and these girls were already emotionally completely dependent on their loverboy and then no longer accessible to friends and parents. Mostly they disappeared from the scene and had no contact with their parents for months. At some point the loverboys would then get the girls into prostitution, using both psychological and physical violence. Often, the girls were told a story of high debts that could only be paid off in this way. Most loverboys had several girls on the hook at the same time, through whom they earned a lot of money. The girls were usually sixteen or seventeen years old, but there were even cases with fourteen-year olds. At that age many were susceptible to such seduction. Moreover, such young girls were popular with the clients and therefore brought in good money - in other words, the right target group for the loverboys in every respect.

Elin was shocked by this kind of pimping. Why was the creativity of people so often transformed into criminal energy? And what ruthlessness was used in the implementation! Elin shook her head; it was also astonishing that the girls would allow themselves to be treated like that. Didn't they have an alternative? Or why did they stay with the guys who were just using them?

She almost blamed herself. Maybe after finding Hanna at her boyfriend's place she should have informed herself more about the situation. Then she would certainly have come across the issue with these loverboys and could have given the parents the appropriate documents so they could have called the police, gotten them involved and everything would have turned out differently. It had not been enough to merely locate the girl; the underlying problem should have been tackled here. This Ali had apparently proceeded exactly as described in the articles. Elin was desperate to find out whether he had previously woven other girls into his web in this manner or whether he might have had other girls turning tricks for him beside Hanna, perhaps in other apartments. In any case, this Ali had been a real pig. They had to find out more about this.

23

Lars was sitting in the pizzeria in Sollentuna again, it had not been possible to delegate today's surveillance. But he had been able to clarify everything else with Tobias regarding the new assignment. In the past, special cases like this invariably led to a discussion with Tobias, as they were beyond their normal scope. Tobias did not want any assignments that were not predictable, not with respect to the outcome or the potential risk. Meanwhile, however, he did not cause any further difficulties. On the one hand, he had come to realize that Lars and Elin were capable of solving such cases, and on the other hand, there had been considerable publicity resulting in a significant increase in business. Everything that was good for the company was worthwhile as far as Tobias was concerned. That's why he had also started to pay a commission if Lars himself landed any assignments. Not wanting to offer this benefit to any of the other employees, he had conferred procuration upon Lars, which made things much easier. Lars could therefore enter into contracts on his own, he only had to inform Tobias. And it was also financially attractive for him, because his salary had increased and now commissions were added on top of that.

Yes, professionally, he was doing well. If only his personal life would go as smoothly. But Lisa never really could warm up to his job. Nevertheless, he still couldn't really understand why she had proven herself so uncompromising. After all, he hadn't had any dangerous cases since she had filed for divorce. Obviously, it was sufficient to know that something like this could happen again at any time. All the same, sometimes he suspected that there were other reasons for the separation from him. He had been waiting for Lisa to show up with another man, but that had not happened yet. Nor could Lars see any indication of this when he picked up the children from her house, and the children had not reported anything in this direction either. Last year, Lisa had made it so difficult for him to live under the same roof together that he wouldn't necessarily cry after her, but he didn't like the fact that they weren't a real family anymore. Having the children with him only every other weekend and on vacation was already a big restriction. Besides, it wasn't nice living alone. He had already started to look around on some dating apps, but he actually wasn't sure if he was ready to start a new relationship yet.

In two months, he would celebrate his 40th birthday. Under normal circumstances, he would have celebrated it on a larger scale, but as it was now, he no longer felt like it. Maybe he'd go out for a beer with a couple of co-workers. Or get a pizza. Well, it didn't have to be pizza. Somehow, they ate a lot of that at work. He looked around the restaurant and wondered if he should order one again today. There were many pizzerias in strategic locations; it was really strange that in eight out of ten cases, they would set up their surveillance post in a pizzeria whenever it wasn't possible to sit in their car and do so.

Once again, he glanced in the direction of the office under surveillance, but nothing was happening there. Perhaps he dared to read further through the documents that the lawyer had sent yesterday? He had already looked through a large part of it the evening before. The lawyer had made copies of the documents from the prosecutor's office and sent them along with the signed contract. This was a massive package with quite a lot of pages, most of them written in a rather complicated way. The preliminary autopsy report left no doubt that Ali Fakhoury had died as a result of the single stab wound; other than that, he had no injuries.

He had died shortly before the ambulance arrived, in other words, while Hanna was with him. The pathologist reported that the knife had been thrust into the chest with a great deal of force. He thought it more likely that a man had delivered this stab but could not necessarily rule out a woman as the perpetrator. This unfortunately did not exclude Hanna as the killer, as she was the only one found at the scene of the crime. Furthermore, as the lawyer had previously pointed out, only her fingerprints were on the knife, which incidentally was taken from the kitchen of the apartment - it was the largest of a six-piece set. Lars would have liked to know if the other knives also had Hanna's prints on them, but the forensic team hadn't examined them. It could be that Hanna had been responsible for cooking meals while they had lived in Tulegatan. If Ali's prints were on the other knives, then it would be a bit suspicious that they were missing on the murder weapon. Anyway, it was likely that all the knives had been washed in the dishwasher, thus wiping away any fingerprints on them. If Hanna had taken out the big knife, then obviously only her fingers had come into contact with it.

The state of the apartment after the crime had clearly indicated an argument had taken place - glasses had been broken, chairs overturned, the table out of place, coffee spilled. Everything fit the prosecutor's interpretation, Lars had to admit to that.

The police had been able to prove that Hanna had taken the subway from Norsborg at 1:08 PM and arrived at Sundbyberg Center at 2:03 PM. The police were called at 2:25 PM. It took about ten minutes to walk from the train station to the apartment in Tulegatan. That gave Hanna a maximum of fifteen minutes to argue with Ali and stab him. Not much, but certainly not impossible. She had perhaps already been angry when she arrived, and then there was a verbal altercation, finally a scuffle, which ended with her grabbing the knife. The police report mentioned that both the espresso machine and the dishwasher had been on - had Ali done this before Hanna arrived?

What had they been arguing about? Lars had a hard time believing the story about the prostitution, but the evidence was really very strong, even though you could put pictures on the internet without actually seeing johns. Elin had called this morning and told him about the loverboy phenomenon. Lars had read about it before but had never had anything directly to do with it. He would have associated the term loverboy with something else. However, it clearly looked like this Ali had driven Hanna into prostitution. She certainly wouldn't have done that on her own. So, supposing it was true and Hanna - which he could understand well – didn't want to give in to it or to continue doing it. She could have left Ali at any time if they couldn't agree. Her parents would have gladly welcomed her back home. Hanna must have known that. Why should she kill him? Of course, an argument could escalate and end up with a knife stabbing, but then it was manslaughter at best, if not self-defense. But then why wouldn't Hanna testify? From his point of view, she could only win by doing so. After all, the truth couldn't be worse than murder. Or had she suffered trauma and therefore could not speak about it?

Nothing else happened in front of the office of the two people he was watching. Lars started leafing through the document package. There was a printout of text messages that Ali had received from Hanna. The first text message on the eve of his death. Hanna had asked when he would be home. The next morning, the day of the deed, she had written, "Ali, honey, where are you? Please answer." There were three red hearts behind it. Sure didn't sound like anger ... And then there was one last text, sent at 12:35 PM, "Ali, I'm worried. Now heading to Tulegatan to find you. Call me please." Again, with a heart and a kissing emoji. It sounded more like Hanna was desperate because Ali hadn't come home. What did all of this mean? That the reason for a dispute had only arisen after they met up in Tulegatan? Was there someone else in the apartment, maybe another girl? Or had Hanna seen anything that made her angry? He would go over the crime scene description once more. Of course, Ali could also have said something that triggered the argument – then, of course, they would not be able to find any clue to indicate this. If that was what had happened, only Hanna could really help them by talking.

A quick look at the street, no, both cars were still there. He flipped to the crime scene description. There were quite a few photos here. Lars couldn't find anything striking. There was no evidence of another person. However, the fingerprints had only been secured on the knife, and no one seemed to have searched for any on the broken glass or broken coffee cup. He had to discuss this with Edvard, it would be really interesting to know who had drunk from it. Only Ali? Or Hanna too? Or possibly a third person? Lars would send him an email, he pulled out his smartphone.

24

lin was back with Paula in the *Offside Sports Bar*. She had texted her last night and asked for a meeting, which Paula had immediately agreed to. Elin preferred to speak to Paula alone, because the presence of her husband would have only inhibited her. And anyway, Elin did not believe that he could contribute much to the enlightenment. Paula didn't look good, she looked tired. Her face was swollen, and the make-up hadn't been able to hide that either.

"It's a bad situation," began Elin. "I can't imagine Hanna doing something like that."

"Hanna didn't do that. She would never do anything like that." Paula was very determined. "I wouldn't even believe it if Hanna said so herself that she had done it."

Elin nodded understandingly. That was the elephant in the room – the big problem. "What does she say? The lawyer says she refuses to talk about everything that has to do with Ali."

"Yes, unfortunately. I don't think she can speak about it."

"Paula, please explain to me what goes on when you meet her. You visit her regularly, don't you?"

"Yes, almost every day," Paula confirmed.

"And what's it like then? I mean, is she happy that you're coming? Is there a conversation? Does she tell anything at all?"

"Well, so ... first of all you have to know that Göran doesn't always come with me. And even if he is really nice to her now, she is more open when it's just the two of us and we are alone. Yes, she is happy, she smiles and hugs me when I come. I then ask her how she is getting along in prison and if she needs anything, things like that. Then she reacts normally. Obviously, she doesn't like it there, she's bored and wants her smartphone, but she can't have that. She usually doesn't like the food either. So, then I'll update her on what's going on at home, what we're doing, how Evelina is doing, who has asked about her. After that we usually just sit there and look at each other, I hold her hand and stroke it..." Paula had tears in her eyes, she looked away.

"But if she's not feeling well there, she should have the need to get out. Does she say anything about that?"

"She's not talking about that. She only nods when I say that we want to bring her back home. I'm sure she wants that too."

"But then she has to do something about it. At least talk about what happened that day. If she did nothing or it was just self-defense, she will be released immediately."

"The lawyer explained that to her several times and we kept repeating it, but she doesn't react at all to that."

"What do you mean by that? How does she behave when you bring up that subject?"

"Well, she no longer looks at us and says nothing more. Sometimes I think she really clamps her lips together so that she doesn't spill anything."

"I understand. How does she act if you change the subject again?"

"Then it takes a moment before she starts talking to us and looking at us again. Sometimes you have to repeat the sentence two or three times before you can even get through to her."

Elin pondered the situation; it was a really difficult one. The only witness didn't help them. "That means she didn't say a word the whole time about her relationship with Ali or what happened on the day of his death? Really absolutely nothing?"

Paula seemed to be thinking. Finally, she shook her head. "No, nothing at all. And we tried again and again. But as soon as you ask something about it, she withdraws and says nothing more. We are now avoiding the issue, despite the fact that the lawyer asked us not to give up."

"Did she say anything about the time when you had no contact?"

Paula shook her head again. "No, we don't even know where she lived after moving out of the Tulegatan apartment."

There was information in the documents that the lawyer had sent them, Elin knew, somewhere in Botkyrka. She was really keen on taking a look at the apartment.

The waiter came with the meal, they had both ordered hamburgers. Elin was hungry, her mouth watered. She quickly reached for her hamburger. Anyway, she didn't have the impression that she could get more out of the conversation with Paula. Unfortunately, it hadn't been as fruitful as she had wanted.

***

Elin was sitting in the conference room, spreading all of Hanna's case papers out on the table when Lars came in. They wanted to update each other about their first results and explore the next steps to take.

"How was your meeting with Hanna's mother?" Lars sat down and placed his coffee mug on the table in front of him.

"Nothing new, she just confirmed what the lawyer said. You can't get anything out of her that's relevant to our case."

Lars sighed. "Too bad. If that doesn't change, we are completely on our own."

"And you?" Elin raised her eyebrows.

"I've looked over the documents carefully." He nodded his head towards documents. "I noticed a few things in doing so. For example, that no fingerprints were searched for on some of the items. There could possibly be traces of a third person there - I am thinking mainly of the coffee cup and the broken glass. I have asked Edvard about this via text message. He replied that we should gather such points first. He has to pass these questions on to the prosecutor's office, and he doesn't want to do that more than once. He's afraid they'll just act stubbornly."

"Got it." Elin reached for her pad. "Should we make a list?"

"For sure. Do you have any points to add to it?"

Elin thought about it. "Well, I don't know about the phone data. The numbers of Hanna and Ali are in the report, so I could of course get the movement data and conversation lists myself, but not in a legal way. Therefore, it might be better to request them officially so that Edvard can then use any results in court. Or what do you think?"

Lars scratched behind his left ear. "That's a good point. On the one hand, it would be safer to go the official way. On the other hand, this will likely set us back in time. I'm afraid we won't get the data that quickly, if at all. The public prosecutor is not obliged to comply with the defense's requests."

"Well, how about this solution - we request the data formally, and I'll still get it myself. Then we don't waste any time and can still refer to the official lists afterwards."

"Great way to solve it." Lars smiled contentedly. "That is what we'll do."

Elin added that to the list. "I would also like to see both the crime scene and the apartment in Botkyrka. Do you think that is possible?"

Lars shrugged his shoulders. "We'll give it a try. That would be good, otherwise we only have the few pictures in the report and the description."

Elin noted it. "It is the first time for me that I have read such a document. You're familiar with them." After all, Lars had worked as a police officer for ten years, when he not only read such reports, but probably also wrote them himself. "I find the report rather sketchy. What do you say as a former cop?"

Lars nodded in confirmation. "You're right. It's like the lawyer said - the police were sure from the beginning that they already had the perpetrator, and therefore they only investigated in this direction; in other words, they only looked for evidence and proof that would confirm the preconceived opinion. Traces that could point to other perpetrators were not even looked for, and no corresponding analyses were carried out. Everything might have been different if Hanna had made a statement, always assuming that she has not killed Ali. It could of course have been self-defense."

"I don't think she killed him," Elin said. "Did you read the text messages that Hanna sent him? They don't sound like she was angry with him, but rather more like she was worried about him. Then she finally finds him and kills him? Doesn't sound plausible to me."

Lars frowned. "Unfortunately, we don't know what a possible dispute was about. Maybe Hanna found out something she didn't know before, for example, that there was another woman. I've read that these loverboys often take advantage of multiple girls at the same time."

"Yes. But then we should find out. That would be a mitigating factor for the judge. After all, Ali took advantage of Hanna and just played his love for her. Anyone would go crazy if that became clear to her."

"On the other hand, Hanna would have all the more reason to spill the beans about her relationship with Ali. Why does she protect him, especially posthumously?"

Elin threw her hands in the air. "Yes, we always come back to the same topic. Hanna's silence. Why doesn't she say anything? I hope we get a chance to talk to her. At least I want to try to get something out of her."

"Yes, Edvard wanted to apply for it. But as long as we have no statement from Hanna, we have to investigate in all directions. There may have been an argument that forced Hanna to self-defense, or there might be a third party involved. These are the two scenarios that would help Hanna. We can leave the scenarios of murder or homicide to the prosecutor. But Elin, let's be clear about one thing - If we are to implicate someone else, our chances are not good. The first 24 hours are decisive for finding a culprit, after that the traces go cold very quickly. We've already lost ten days, so it's going to be tough."

Elin grinned. "Tough, but not impossible. The question is, who else can be considered a perpetrator? If there was a second girl or even more in Ali's life, they are also candidates, after all, they might have found out about Hanna. Then there would be other pimps or loverboys from the milieu with whom he might have had a fight. The report also said that drugs were found in the apartment in Botkyrka. These could have led to conflicts with dealers. We have a lot to clarify."

Lars tilted his head to the side and said triumphantly, "I have another candidate. And we should definitely check him out."

Who was he talking about? Someone specific? No one else was mentioned in the report. Elin looked at

Lars questioningly: "Okay, I'm at a loss here. Who are you talking about?"

"Isn't it obvious? Ali first persuades Hanna to move in with him, and when we find her, she refuses to go back home. Then he forces her into prostitution. Hanna's father is prone to violence - if he could have figured out what was going on, I can very well imagine an escalated meeting with Ali."

"Shit", it hit Elin. "I hadn't thought of that. But then he could clear Hanna. Göran wouldn't want Hanna to be convicted of his crime."

"Well, when you weigh the potential penalties, it's a little more understandable. Hanna gets a maximum of four years in juvenile prison for murder, while Göran can be sentenced to up to eighteen years in prison. For manslaughter it would be at least six years, for Hanna probably only one or two years. Therefore, you could say that Hanna will be free after a very short time and will not have to endure much in a juvenile prison, whereas this would be a major blow for her father."

Elin pursed her lips. "You're right. That fits. Moreover, Göran might think that it would be quite good for Hanna if she were to be taken out of the picture for a while. That way she couldn't do drugs or prostitute herself. But then why are we being contracted? He could just wait and see."

"Maybe Paula is the initiative. Or Göran sees an opportunity to negotiate the sentence down to manslaughter or self-defense in order to reduce the sentence or even acquit Hanna."

"Yes, but he does take the risk that we will find traces that indicate him."

Lars shrugged. "Yes, I do not want to say that Göran is the perpetrator. I just think that we cannot rule him out as a suspect and therefore we have to check him out. If he's got an alibi at the time of the crime, then we can close that line of investigation."

"Fine, should I do it?"

"Nah, let me do that. You take care of the phone records first and send our list to the lawyer. I'll go see Göran and Ali's parents." Lars got up.

"Okay." Elin remained seated. She was still stunned by Lars' theory. That would be awesome. It could even be that Hanna was there at the crime and therefore was silent. If her father had killed Ali and she had witnessed it, it would provoke within her a conflict of emotions. That could even explain why she was not talking. What a case this was!

She put the documents together. Once she'd sent the list to Edvard, she would go to the phone servers. Let's see what came out of it. She would also check Göran's number right away, at least that gave her a first clue as to where he had been on the crucial day.

ars turned to the next page of the newspaper, there in the local section of Stockholm was a report about a fifteen-year-old girl who sat completely alone in front of the Reichstag and waged a three-week school strike. Her name was Greta Thunberg and she was protesting on behalf of saving the climate. "Politicians have to put ecology before economy," she was quoted as saying. The picture showed the girl crouching on the cobblestones with a large sign next to her. It read: "School strike for the climate." She would spend every day of school here until the Reichstag election in September. Lars was impressed, the girl looked younger than fifteen, but was apparently determined to express her opinion. He wasn't quite convinced that a school strike was the right thing to do; after all, Greta only harmed herself by staying away from classes, even though she was apparently learning from her textbooks while demonstrating. Still, the action caused a sensation. The article cited other students who planned to join the strike next week. It remained to be seen what results Greta's action would trigger. He was skeptical that it would really change anything, but the girl showed backbone, you had to give her that much. He thought of Hanna, who was just sixteen and now in prison. What a difference. One struggled to save the world, and the other obviously didn't even want to help herself.

In four years, his older girl would be fifteen - which way would she go? He wanted to do everything possible to prevent her from going in the same direction as Hanna. However, he wasn't entirely sure yet whether Greta was a desirable role model. Yes, if Greta were his daughter, he would of course support her, as her parents apparently did. But this path was certainly not easy. Yes, he would be most satisfied with something in between these two poles, the golden middle. Fortunately, he still had four years' time left, and it was three years longer for Olivia. Which also meant that if Greta and the scientists she referred to were right, his two daughters would be even more affected by the effects of climate change than Greta herself. The predictions did not sound good, and this year's summer seemed to give a glimpse of what the future would be like - dry and hot, coupled with low water tables and forest fires. One could only hope that the predictions would not come true, be it because the calculations were wrong or because Greta actually moved the world to change.

He thoughtfully put the newspaper aside and looked at his watch. Quarter to eleven. He should be at the construction site in half an hour, that's when Göran had his lunch break. Lars had been pondering for a while how he could check Göran's alibi without asking him, but he hadn't found a better way. In other cases, he had pretended to be a tax officer and called the suspect's payroll company. There you could purport an alleged error in the system and check the presence at the job for a certain month. But it was still too early for that, because the sick leave notifications for single days were usually not settled until the following month, this ploy would not work now. Nor did he see any way of finding out where Göran was working at the time in question or the names of his colleagues through the company. For reasons of data protection, this information was not allowed to be provided. So, he would ask Göran himself, and he didn't intend to use the word alibi. Still, that could be uncomfortable. Talking to Ali's parents would certainly not be pleasant either, he had already found out where they lived, which was in Södertälje. He would go there after lunch in the hopes of meeting someone there in the afternoon. There was little point in calling beforehand, they would probably just say they didn't want to speak to him. It was better to confront the parents personally and spontaneously, preferably individually.

The construction site where Göran was now working was in Danderyd. There the *Mörby Center* was being expanded and renovated. Göran was one of the tradesmen who built the new parking garage. It never ceased to amaze Lars that there were so many shopping malls being developed, especially since there was the new Mall of Scandinavia next to the new *Friends Arena*, which was after all the largest shopping mall in the Stockholm area. But there seemed to be an almost unlimited need; in the north alone the *Täby Center* had just been expanded and now the Mörby *Center* was added.

The trip to Danderyd went quickly. Since the *Norra Länken* highway and tunnels had been completed, the traffic situation had improved considerably. The long traffic jams were a thing of the past, at least outside of peak hours. That's why it only took half an hour to get from the office in Södermalm *to Mörby Center*.

Lars parked in the provisional north parking lot and went through the underpass under the E18 to the parking garage under construction. Large walls had been erected to separate the construction site from the footpath. Göran had said that at the roundabout before the entrance to the parking garage there was a blue construction trailer where they could meet.

The construction trailer was unmistakable; a group of men in working pants and yellow reflective vests was standing in front of it. When Lars got closer, he recognized Göran among them. He had already recognized him and was coming towards him, a yellow helmet under his left arm, a lunch box in his right hand.

"*Hej* Göran. Thank you for making time for this. "

"No problem," answered Göran. "But I don't have much time and I still have to eat."

"It won't take long. Where can we talk?" Lars looked around questioningly.

Göran pointed past the roundabout to the street that led away from the center. "There is a small piece of forest with a playground over there. We can sit on a bench there."

"Great." Lars turned and followed Göran. They crossed the Mörbyleden and walked a little way through the trees. It was pleasant here in the shade because the sun was burning and there was almost no wind. The playground had a full range of playground equipment, most of them made of wood, which fit well here. At the moment there was only one woman with two small children on the square. Between the spacious sandpit and the swings were two frames with benches and tables, where they both sat down. Göran unpacked his sandwiches and started to eat.

"My colleague has already spoken to your wife," started Lars. "That's why I wanted to meet you too."

Göran nodded as he continued chewing.

"How did you find out about Hanna's arrest?"

"The police called us. Hanna is still a minor, so they needed our consent to interrogate her."

"I understand. Did they call you or Paula?"

"They tried the two of us, but they reached me first. It was a Monday and Paula usually works there until eight in the evening. She had her cell phone turned off while working, so they couldn't reach her. But I always start at seven and finish at four. My cell phone is always on mute, and when I picked it up at the end of the shift, the first thing I saw were the messages, and I immediately got in touch with the police. It was quite a shock; they didn't tell me at the beginning why Hanna had been arrested. I only found out when I arrived at the station."

Well, if that was true, Göran had a solid alibi. Ali was stabbed to death around 2:15 p.m., so Göran typically would have been at the construction site.

"Was it also here you worked that day?"

"Yes. I've been working at this construction site for a year now."

"Do you drive here or how did you get to the police?"

"*Nej*, man, the parking fees are very expensive here, it would cost too much. I am going by bus from Solna. I took the subway to the police. At first I thought it would be better to change clothes beforehand, but then I would have lost even more time. So, I went straight from here to there. Not that it did any good, because she didn't say a word."

"What? That Monday she hadn't said anything at all? I thought just not about the case?"

Göran took another bite of his sandwich, the smell of salami wafted over. "Not a single word. She hardly looked at me."

"And when did she talk to you for the first time?"

Göran swallowed the last bite and wiped his mouth with the back of his hand. "That was the next day. There we went together, so Paula and I. Then she greeted us and told us that she was treated well. However, when we asked what happened the day before, there was radio silence again." He shook his head slowly. "I don't know what's going on with the girl. First, she runs away from home, then she breaks off the contact, and now this.

"Do you believe that she killed this Ali? I mean, because she snapped or in self-defense."

"Not really. Hanna was always on the shy side and never violent. Sure, she argued with her sister, but only verbally, she never hit her. Evelina could become more physical, but Hanna only defended herself, never hit back. But..." He closed his eyes and lowered his head. Quietly he continued, "...but I never thought she would take drugs or get involved with men for money either. I still can't believe that. Somehow that's not our Hanna."

Lars waited; maybe more would come.

Göran swallowed hard, then looked up. His light gray eyes bored into Lars'. "I really hope she didn't do this, even though she might have had reason to do so. The guy tricked her into all this. If she had come to me, I would have beaten that guy black and blue..."

"Did you see Ali again?"

"No, just the one time when we wanted to get Hanna back. He didn't say much, kept out of it. But our daughter really wanted to stay there. You can see how that ended up."

"Then who found out that Hanna had moved out of Tulegatan?"

"That was Paula, she went there again and talked to this Ali briefly. Would have been better if I had gone. I would have beaten out of him where Hanna is."

"Why didn't you do that afterwards?"

"I've been thinking about it, believe me." He laughed bitterly. "But what good would it do? Hanna didn't want to get away from him. I was hoping that after a while she would come to her senses herself. Instead, she is in prison now." He shook his head in disbelief and then looked up. "I have to go back now. Do you have any more questions?"

"No. If you can think of anything else that could be of importance, you have my number."

They rose and went back through the trees to the street. Lars had the strong feeling that Göran had nothing to do with the crime. He had sounded authentic and Lars didn't think he was that good of an actor. But of course, that didn't mean that he could be completely excluded from the group of suspects.

***

The drive to Södertälje was no problem, during the day the route was rarely congested, and the highway had three lanes in each direction for most of the way. Lars used the time and called Elin to let her know about the conversation with Göran. Elin was disappointed that Göran was not a suspect after all, she had probably fallen a little in love with the idea. She was busy hacking the phone server.

The address of the Fakhourys was easy to find, they lived in a residential complex called Tveta in the southwest of Södertälje. In the long, eight-floor building Lars quickly found the right entrance, but obviously nobody was at home, at least there was no reaction to his ringing the doorbell. He sat in his Volvo and waited. Luckily, he had found a place in the shade. Unfortunately, there was no parking space that allowed him to watch the front door, so he couldn't see from here if anyone was entering the house. He checked his watch again, now it was half past two. If he was unlucky, he would have to wait until five or longer. He would try again in half an hour.

When he rang the bell the next time, the buzzer went. He looked through the directory next to the mailboxes, the Fakhourys lived on the seventh floor, the elevator was waiting. When he reached the top, he rang the doorbell. After a little while he heard footsteps, someone was standing behind the door, probably peering through the spyhole. Lars tried to smile friendly. As a reward, the door was tentatively opened a little. A small, somewhat plump woman with a light blue headscarf and a brown apron peeked through it. "What do you want?"

"My name is Lars Olsson. First of all, I would like to express my deep condolences on Ali's death."

The woman sniffed. She was carefully made up, her face was almost white, her cheeks were pink, her eyebrows were drawn with a pencil, her eyes were outlined with thick eyeliner, and her lips were deep red. Still, he didn't think she was pretty, she had a big nose and rough features. This had to be Ali's mother Shadiyah, she was forty-eight according to the population registers. She looked at him with big dark eyes. "You friend of Ali?"

"I am investigating his death and would like to ask you some questions about Ali."

"You cop? We said everything already." She looked at him suspiciously.

"No, I'm a private investigator. Can I come in for a moment?"

The woman kept a straight face; she seemed to be thinking. Lars knew that his size was often intimidating, maybe he should have sent Elin here after all. He put on the most winning smile he had.

"It really won't take long."

She opened the door and raised her right arm towards the hall. "Okay."

It smelled of food, infused with oriental spices. The woman led him into the kitchen, which was simply furnished, but rather cluttered: pots and pans hung everywhere, on numerous shelves stood spice mixtures and jars with dried herbs. On the stove a closed pot simmered next to a pan in which some sort of meatballs was roasting. That's where the smell came from. Lars followed the woman's inviting hand gesture and sat down at the small table.

"I have to cook, my husband coming soon," she said. She lifted the lid of the pot, checking it, was obviously satisfied and put it back. Then she turned the meatballs with a wooden spatula. Finally, she narrowed her eyebrows at him. "What you want to know?"

She didn't seem to have any intention of offering him anything, so Lars began, "Has Ali had problems with anyone lately? Problems that could have led to an argument?"

The woman sighed loudly. "My Ali was good boy. He didn't do anything to anyone. But hanging with wrong people."

That was an interesting statement. He waited to see if she would say more about it, then asked, "What kind of people were they?"

She turned to him and shrugged her shoulders. "What should I say? I don't know them. But everyone says they're no good. Sometimes dangerous. You must be very careful. They deal with drugs. They collect money everywhere. You don't pay, they cause problems. Big problems."

"What did Ali have to do with them? Did he owe them money?"

She shook her head. "He worked for them."

Lars was not really surprised; he had been wondering all the time how a young man like Ali could have driven such an expensive car. And his lifestyle was not exactly frugal in other respects either.

"What did he do? What kind of work was it?"

"I'm not sure. Ali not talk much about it. He said not dangerous, but I don't believe." She seemed to be getting nervous, she ran her hands over her apron. She looked at him helplessly and turned back to the stove.

"He must have said something. Did he deal with drugs?"

"I just know he drove around much, to restaurants and nightclubs. He said he not do drugs and not sell them either."

The door was unlocked outside in the corridor. Lars heard someone come in and walk down the hall with heavy steps. A deep voice called something in Arabic. The woman answered and turned to the kitchen entrance. She told Lars, "This my husband."

Lars rose to greet the man who had just appeared in the doorway. He was medium in size but very strong, had bushy eyebrows, a bald head and a strong mustache. He stopped dead when he saw Lars.

Before Lars could say anything, he released a tirade in Arabic aimed at his wife. She answered with short sentences. Finally, the man turned his dark eyes to Lars.

"Who do you work for?"

"For the defense lawyer."

The man took a step towards Lars. "The bitch's lawyer? Who killed our son?"

"There are still significant ..." He got no further. The man took a step to the side and gestured to the door. "Out. Get out of my apartment. We have nothing to talk to you about."

Lars nodded. "Yes, I'm going. I had just..."

"Out. Now. Before I help you."

Lars raised his hands and went from the kitchen into the hallway. The man followed him.

"Thanks for letting me speak to you," Lars shouted to the woman. "My condolences again."

The man pushed him to the apartment door. "Out now. Leave and never come back."

The door slammed behind him. Lars stood in the stairwell and took a deep breath. The man had been really close to attacking him. Not that Lars would have been afraid of getting into a fight but beating up the victim's father just didn't seem like a good idea. And wouldn't take him a step further. Still, he was glad to have been here. The mother's few sentences had been very revealing. That gave them a new approach. He was sure that Elin would like it. Lars smiled and pressed the button for the elevator.

The phone records were a mess. At least Ali's were. With the others it was quite manageable. Getting the data was no problem, just a little time consuming, because the phones were registered with different providers and Elin had to hack several different servers.

Göran's phone had been logged in near *Mörby Center* where he was working on the day of the crime. In the late afternoon he had been at the police station on *Kungsholmen* – this all matched his statement to Lars. Unfortunately. Elin had to admit to herself that she didn't like the man, furthermore he had treated Hanna badly and seemed to be violent in general. So, it would have been satisfying for her to nail this on him. But that was not the point, she could not choose the perpetrator. It would only have been nice to have found a suspect so quickly on whom one could have focused the investigation. But he seemed out of the question. Unless he had left his cell phone at work, gone to Ali's house and picked it up again after the murder. But that would mean that he had planned the whole thing coldly; and then put on a real good show for Lars to show his innocence. She didn't think he was capable of all that, he seemed to be more of a man of passion. Well, she wouldn't completely cross him off the list, but Lars was right, Göran was probably not the perpetrator.

Hanna had two telephones, one for private use and one for the johns. On the first one there were almost exclusively conversations with Ali, on the second one, incoming calls had been received from many different numbers. That made sense. This phone had not moved from the apartment in Botkyrka, that also matched up. The private cell phone, on the other hand, showed that Hanna had been away a lot on certain days. As far as Elin could determine, she had been to shopping malls, restaurants and the beach. On the day of Ali's death, she had spent the morning in the apartment in Botkyrka and had gone to Sundbyberg in Tulegatan at noon, just as she had announced in the text message to Ali. But there was something interesting as well. Hanna had dialed another number that morning, which was not in her call data. Hanna had already looked for it on the internet, but the number was not registered, probably a prepaid card. She thought about whether she should just call there or whether she should get the phone data right away. Hanna had made a short phone call with the subscriber, which must have had something to do with Ali's absence. This contact could end up being an interesting lead.

Yeah, and then there was Ali's phone. Lots of tracking data and a mass of phone calls with a large number of numbers. So, she wanted to bring Carl back on board. However, after Carl had gone into business for himself a while ago, he was charging pretty hefty prices for his special services. She would check with Lars whether they had the budget for it. In any case, she needed the right software to somehow match the tracking data with the telephone calls, by hand it would take days and be extremely tedious. She would of course be able to pick the geodata and calls from the lists for a selected time, but to get the complete picture of the last weeks, she needed automation.

Anyway, she had already done the work for the day Ali was killed, and the result was a bit strange. While Ali had otherwise made a lot of phone calls every day, there was not a single call on that Monday, and also on the Sunday evening before that nothing was recorded. Hanna had called him twice on Monday morning, but these conversations had ended up in the mailbox. Otherwise zilch. And the tracking data were also a surprise. Elin had expected that Ali had spent the night and the morning before his death in the apartment in Tulegatan, possibly having fun with another girl. This would have explained the silence on his phone and would also have been a plausible reason for a fight with Hanna. But no, he had gone to Tulegatan only right before Hanna did. Prior to this he had been at another address in Enskede the whole time. That was in the south of Stockholm, there were restaurants, nightclubs, shops and of course lots of private apartments - unfortunately Elin couldn't narrow down exactly where Ali had been there. Maybe he had met a girl there, spent the night with her and after a long morning in bed he had gone to Tulegatan, possibly together with the girl, and had been surprised by Hanna there. Although ... then he hadn't read Hanna's text messages, had he? Elin checked the time of Hanna's last text message to Ali. It was 12:35 PM. She compared this with the geodata on Ali's mobile phone - he had been in Enskede until 12:50 PM, then logged in on Tulegatan at 1:15 PM. Elin opened Google Maps and entered the two addresses, and it took twenty minutes by car, which was a fit. She leafed through the police report, yes, Ali's car had been parked in Tulegatan. Apparently, they had not evaluated the GPS, but it was to be assumed that Ali had covered this last bit in his Audi. This meant that he had already received the text message from Hanna in which she announced that she was going to Tulegatan. A quarter of an hour later he set off to go there as well. Why? Was it a reaction to the text message? Did he want to meet Hanna there? But then he could have called her back or sent a short reply, like: "All right, darling, I'll meet you there." But he hadn't. Or did he want to give the impression that he had spent the night there well-behaved and alone? Then he must have said goodbye to his girl in Enskede and rushed to Sundbyberg to arrive there before Hanna. Maybe he wanted to pretend being surprised by her and that's why he hadn't answered Hanna. Yes, that was plausible.

But then what happened? Ali had obviously been there on time, almost an hour before Hanna. He could have arranged everything to fit his scenario. Having had too much to drink in the evening, hangover in the morning, stayed in bed for a long time - that would have been a good explanation for his inaccessibility. Elin looked at the police report again. The crime scene photos showed the chaos in the living room, but the bedroom was completely untouched, the bed was made, everything was tidy. Had Elin been in Ali's shoes, she would have trashed the place, as if he had slept there in an intoxicated state. The photo of Ali didn't match either, he was fully dressed in jeans and a polo shirt, he even had his sneakers on when he lay dead on the floor. Elin would have thought that he would have rather faced Hanna in pajamas and a bathrobe. Then he could have said that he had just woken up and therefore hadn't answered before. No, he had left the bedroom untouched and had not changed. Then came Hanna - what excuse had he given her? Elin couldn't think of anything sensible. Maybe that's why they had an argument, if there had been an argument between them in the first place. Hanna had been angry because he hadn't answered, and she had been worried while he sat calmly in the apartment. But that didn't mean you pulled out a knife and stabbed him, did it? No, Elin was convinced that it would have taken more for it to happen. Had Ali told her that there was another girl? Did he want to change her from number one to number two? Just have her earn money? Of course, that would be grounds for an argument. But Hanna could have just said no and left him, or did Ali have her in his hands somehow? Was there any leverage that kept her from just turning her back on him?

Elin realized that she was stuck here. They needed more information. It would help to find out what Ali had done in Enskede. And if there was another girl, they had to find her. It would be an important step to confirm this hypothesis and find out more details. Maybe Ali had told this girl why he suddenly had to leave so quickly. On the other hand - if this girl existed, why hadn't she attempted any contact after Ali's death? It had been almost two weeks now. If it hadn't been a one-night stand, the girl must have wondered why Ali hadn't gotten in touch. But if it was only a one-night stand, there was no reason for Ali to confront Hanna with it. Elin noticed how she was going in circles. Maybe all this was wrong, and Ali hadn't read the text message from Hanna and had gone to Tulegatan by chance. Either with or without his companion that night. And then Hanna suddenly showed up.

Regardless, the other girl was the key; if she existed, she could provide important information. Elin would check Ali's phone records carefully; her number must be there.

***

They met again in the conference room. Lars talked about his mission in Södertälje and Elin presented the results of the telephone evaluation together with her thoughts. She outlined the three explanations for Ali's activities on Monday on the flipchart, along with the respective discrepancies.

Lars listened attentively, then he smiled. "Yes, your scenarios sound convincing, I don't know which one is the most likely. As you say yourself, in every version there is at least one detail that doesn't fit in. But I agree with you on one thing: We need more facts, whether from Hanna or through our work."

"How about some extra money so I can hire Carl?"

"I have to check this with the lawyer, we hadn't talked about that and the contract says that all extra expenses are subject to the client's approval. If you've already sent him the list, I can check on that right now."

"No, I was still waiting. Which was good, because I came up with a few more points to add."

"Okay, like what?"

Elin pulled out her notebook and read out the inquiries to the prosecution. "Well, we already had the fingerprints of a possible third person on the coffee cup and the broken glass, then the official telephone data and the inspection of the two apartments. I would also like to see if Hanna's and Ali's cell phones have social media apps, Messenger, Instagram, WhatsApp and so on. Because I can't get to that otherwise. I'd also like to know where Ali's Audi was driven in the last 24 hours before his death. The GPS should tell."

Elin looked at Lars, who nodded. "Very good. Add all of those. I also have something else – the toxicological report is still missing from the autopsy report, I would like to remind them of that. I am also interested in Ali's financial situation and employment relationship, there is nothing about that in the police report. His job seems to have been somewhat obscure, possibly illegal. Provided that he really had another job besides his 'loverboy job'. The more we find out about it, the better."

Elin jotted down the points, slowly the list took shape. "Okay, I'll send this to Edvard and ask about the visit to Hanna."

"Wait a minute." Lars leaned forward. "Please send me the list and also a picture of your scenarios, then I will forward everything to the lawyer including the question about the costs for Carl. I don't think it's such a good idea to send several e-mails in parallel."

"That's true." Elin nodded.

"Then we will meet again the day after tomorrow. Earlier, of course, if something exciting happens before then." Lars got up. "*Hejdå*."

"See you." Elin opened her laptop.

September 2018

27

ars was sitting at his desk. He looked at his watch, it was just a little past 11 AM, almost time for lunch. He heard his cell phone ring and pulled it from his jacket. It was the lawyer.

"Hello Edvard."

"Hello, Lars. It seems you have my number stored on your phone."

"You never know when you'll need them." Lars smiled.

"Good. Yesterday you sent me an e-mail with some questions."

"Right."

"I just talked to the D.A., and I went over the whole thing with her. So, first the good news. Elin may visit Hanna, even several times. The prosecutor will authorize her, which means that it should be possible starting tomorrow. You wanted it to be Elin who talks to Hanna, right?"

"Yeah, that's right, I think she can crack her better than me. That's great, thanks." Lars thought of another case where Elin had visited a traumatized little girl for many months. In Elin's presence the child had smiled for the first time and finally uttered her first sentence. Elin had empathy, and you could feel that.

"I wish you good luck, it would be a great success if Hanna started talking."

"Please don't get your hopes up," Lars said. "It's just a try."

"Yes, I know." The lawyer cleared his throat. "Then to the other points. The D.A. wanted the list sent to her by e-mail, so I'll do that now. They want to check how much effort each item involves. They will set up an order of priority in which the responsible officials will try to work through everything. To be honest, I do not think we will get everything delivered, and it may take a while, possibly several weeks, before they deliver what they see worth investigating. I know this from other cases. But it's positive that the D.A. is getting engaged in this at all and not blocking everything out right away."

"Does this mean that the prosecution is not so sure about the murder charge after all?"

"Well, I wouldn't read too much into that. She is cooperative - I know her from other trials, she is fair and wants to give the defense a chance. It is also possible that she herself has noticed how one-sided the investigative process has been so far. That doesn't look so good in front of the judges, and this way she can at least refer to our list and show that other avenues were also pursued."

"Okay, I see. How about our request for the extra budget?"

"Yes, that's no problem, as long as it's within the parameters you set. Oh, I meant to tell you. Please don't tell me in writing if you obtain information by non-legal means or do anything that is not 100% legal. The resulting findings will not be admissible in court, and it is better that there is no written evidence of this. Please, only verbal, okay?"

"Yeah, no problem. Sorry."

"No, it's not an issue. Would only lead to consequences in extreme cases. But it's better to avoid that kind of thing from the start."

"We will comply. Thanks."

"Well, I guess that clears everything up, doesn't it? Oh, wait, I got one more good thing. The D.A. said the toxicology report came back and she's sending it to me today. I'll forward it directly to you. She hadn't read it yet, so I don't know what it says."

"Great, I'll read through it." Maybe something interesting came out of it, but Lars did not have too much hope. Obviously, Ali hadn't been poisoned, and since drugs had been found in the apartment anyway, it wouldn't be all that surprising if Ali had been high.

"What about the two apartments, Tulegatan and Botkyrka, can we go there?"

"Oh, that's right, I forgot. In theory, yes, but only with me and someone from the police. I am allowed to enter, and then I am permitted to bring someone with me, a policeman making sure that we don't tamper with anything. She'll arrange a date for us. I'll contact you as soon as I have it."

"Sounds good."

They took their leave. Lars got up and went over to Elin's office, he wanted to inform her about the news right away.

***

Thoughtfully Lars leaned back. The toxicology report was of little help to them. Yes, Ali had been using drugs regularly, that had been shown by the analysis of his hair, but at the time of his death he had been completely sober, not even alcohol was detectable in his blood. This did not exactly indicate that he had been partying the night before his death. Of course, you could have fun without drugs, maybe he had had extensive sex. On the other hand, the time of death was around noon, there would be no residual alcohol left if Ali had only had a few beers the night before. Either he had had fun with a girl, or it was business, whereby the one did not have to exclude the other. Maybe he had gotten his hooks into a new girl. But Elin hadn't found any signs of another girl yet. However, the contact didn't have to be obvious from the phone lists, maybe the communication was running via WhatsApp or some other messenger service.

They needed more information about Ali. But how to get it? As long as the D.A. didn't give them access to Ali's smartphone, the phone calls were all they had. Or should he try again with Ali's family? The father was not an option, the mother probably wouldn't talk to him anymore, but Ali could have brothers and sisters. Lars went on the Internet. There was no one else registered at the parents' apartment. Maybe the siblings were underage and therefore not listed. The parents were in their fifties, so there could still be children under eighteen. Otherwise there were Fakhourys in Södertälje, Tumba, Solna and Upplands-Väsby, and even further away from Stockholm. Some dropped out because of being the wrong age, but there were still five left, who were between 18 and 30 years old and could be potential siblings of Ali. He would try his luck and call these five. Maybe there was some new information. For now, he first forwarded the tox report to Elin.

28

Hanna went into her cell; the guard locked the door behind her. She lay down on the bed. She pulled her legs up, reached around with her arms and stared at the wall. Everything was so meaningless. Now her parents had hired the detectives again. She had just met the woman; Elin was her name. Again, the same questions her parents and the lawyer had asked. Didn't they understand that she didn't want to talk about it? It was nobody's business what Ali and she did, she wanted to keep it to herself. There was nothing to tell, it would just be dragging it in the mud. Then there was all this talk about how it would save her. Saving herself a few years in juvenile hall. So what? She didn't care what happened to her. Her life was ruined anyway. Without Ali, it was all meaningless. She cried softly to herself.

After a while she sniveled and wiped off her tears with the back of her hand. This Elin had been nice, that's why she had shaken her hand and spoke a few words with her at the beginning. But when the questions came to Ali, she hadn't listened anymore and retreated into herself. Why didn't anyone understand her? She didn't want to start over, she wanted to go back to her little world where she could think about the time with Ali. She wished she could turn back time, be back in the apartment in Tulegatan or even in Botkyrka. Yes, she hadn't liked to have sex with the other men, it had been disgusting. But Ali had always balanced it out and spoiled her so much, her days off with him had been great. She remembered how she had been on the beach with him and how the other girls had looked enviously. She would never have believed that a man like Ali would fall in love with her. How happy she'd been. She would gladly sleep with other men again, and without a word of complaint, if only she could get Ali back. She just had her memories, her cell phone with the many photos had been taken away from her by the police, and she had also had to hand over Ali's beautiful ring when she was taken into custody. She couldn't even get her clothes from their apartment; her parents were not allowed in there. So, they had brought her the black jogging suit from home, not really her favorite outfit and unfortunately no clothing that reminded her of Ali, but still better than the prison clothes she had been forced to wear on the first day. She had nothing here that she had gotten from Ali. She only had her memories. She closed her eyes.

Lunch was almost ready, then the library cart came. The food was disgusting, all that instant meal shit. And she didn't want to read. She didn't want to talk to the other inmates either, even the hour outside she spent alone. The only thing she had tried so far was the TV game shows, that distracted her. The small TV was hanging over her bed.

29

Elin was deeply disappointed, the visit with Hanna had not yielded anything. She pushed open the door to Lars' office.

He lifted his eyes from the PC. "How did it go?"

"Like shit", Elin spat out and then plopped on the chair in frustration.

Lars nodded understandingly. "I didn't really expect anything different. Didn't she say anything at all?"

"It was just like with her parents. She greeted me, I introduced myself and asked her what it was like in custody, she complained about the food, otherwise it was okay. Then I slowly started to talk about her trial, and then she shut down. She didn't look at me or say a word. As if she hadn't been there at all. When I tried to talk about another topic, she didn't react either. So I talked about the parents, then about school and finally about her friend Klara - zero reaction."

"I understand that you are disappointed, but I honestly couldn't imagine that you would be able to accomplish anything with a single conversation. You will need several attempts, and even then, you may not succeed. When are you going back?"

"Tomorrow morning. I signed up for every day this week. But what do I do if tomorrow she doesn't talk to me at all, even about unrelated subjects?"

Lars shrugged his shoulders. "Hang in there. Every meeting is a new chance."

"Great. I'm thrilled." Elin obviously had had high expectations of the conversation with Hanna. She scratched the back of her head. "Maybe I started off the wrong way. I thought I could motivate her to make a new start, that is to get an acquittal and then begin a new life. But she didn't seem interested."

"I assume the parents have tried the same approach."

"Yeah, probably. And I, the dumbass that I am, sang the same song. It was bound to fail. But what else could I lure her with?" She looked at Lars expectantly.

"Good question. What else could she possibly care about? If not to improve her own situation?"

Elin spread her arms. "There is nothing else in her life. Ali is dead, she has no contact with Klara, and her parents don't seem important to her."

"You could tell her about the evil loverboys."

Elin stared at him. Finally, she nodded and said: "Yes, I could claim that Ali had a second girl and that he had cheated on Hanna with this girl the night before he died. Even though I have no proof of this. And that he was just taking advantage of her. But - honestly, either she already knows that and that was the reason for her argument, or she doesn't know anything about it and won't buy it from me without powerful evidence. Besides, this way I run the risk of her not wanting to see me at all."

Lars frowned. "Yes, you're right, this should probably be the last attempt, and only if we have sufficient evidence. So, let's wait with that. What else could we try? You could talk to her about something else, just try to get her to talk. Clothes, movies, what young girls are interested in..."

"And then not mention her relationship with Ali and his death?"

Lars nodded.

"But her parents are already doing that, they have given up on talking about Ali. And they're not getting any information that's gonna help us."

"Well, you're not supposed to do that forever and ever. Talk to her at the next three meetings about such trivial things, and then try to approach the subject of Ali cautiously, through the back door, so to speak."

Elin pricked up her mouth. "Yes, I can try that. I will prepare myself accordingly and call Klara again, she must have a few topics that the two discussed. Thanks, Lars. Good idea."

"My pleasure, I hope it works. And if it doesn't, please don't blame yourself. Maybe nobody can crack this Hanna."

"I know, but we don't have much else to go on. Or has the lawyer contacted you?"

"Yes, we can look at the two apartments tomorrow. The other points are still to be decided."

"At least this is something. What time?"

"At 2 PM."

"Shit, I'll be with Hanna."

"Then I'll do it alone. Are you okay with that?"

Elin nodded reluctantly. "I think so. Can you take pictures?"

Lars nodded.

"Then we can go through them together afterwards."

"Sure." Lars reached for his notebook. "I have another piece of information. I tracked down one of Ali "s sisters. Her name is Saidah, she's two years older than Ali, lives in Tumba, works as a hairdresser. I got hold of her earlier, she wasn't very talkative, but she finally told me that Ali always hangs around with a friend she doesn't like very much. His name is

Mehmed, she didn't know his last name. Did that name come up anywhere on your record, like phone numbers?"

Elin shook her head. "No, but there are many numbers with prepaid cards, maybe one belongs to this Mehmed. I could call the most frequently listed numbers."

"Do that. And let me know as soon as you find this Mehmed."

"Okay." Elin got up and strolled into her office.

***

Elin hung up the phone. The guy didn't want to reveal his name. His number clearly appeared most frequently in Ali's phone list, both incoming and outgoing calls. The two had talked to each other at least once a day. Furthermore, Hanna had dialed this number before she went to Tulegatan on the day of the crime. She had spoken briefly with this man. From the voice, Elin thought he was the same age as Ali. He could well be this Mehmed. But how could she verify it if the guy didn't disclose his name? She could, of course, retrieve his call data and geodata from the server, perhaps this would give her a clue to his address, which she could then check on the spot. That way, they'd also have the advantage of finding the guy right away.

No sooner said than done. First thing Elin found out was which phone company the number belonged to. Halebop. They were with Telia, the biggest operator. She knew the server like the back of her hand.

An hour and a few clicks later she had the data. She sent it to Carl, who had already obtained Ali's movement profile and phone data from her and now compared the phone calls with his whereabouts. Now he could do the same with the files of this suspected Mehmed and also check where the two of them had been together and where they actually had traveled to. She should have the results by the next morning at the latest, Carl usually worked quickly.

ars was monitoring the house in Hammarvägen, in the Jakobsberg district. This part of town was north of Lisa's house, maybe five miles from the place where he had lived with her and the children until not so long ago. Here, in Hammarvägen, Mehmed, Ali's friend, lived. Elin had done the groundwork yesterday. She had looked through the mailboxes in the hallway, and lo and behold, there was a Mehmed Ghannam. Although he was not registered here, he had his name on one of the mailboxes and on one of the doors on the fourth floor. The telephone records showed that he stayed overnight in this house practically all the time. In addition, he had spent a lot of time together with Ali, yes, Ali had even been here with him from time to time. The previous evening, Elin had waited until 11 PM until Mehmed finally arrived home. She had identified him because he had opened the correct mailbox, and after a while the light had gone on in the corresponding apartment. Elin had managed to take a photo of him and attach a transmitter to his car. Mehmed drove a black Porsche Cayenne with red leather seats, which was also registered in his name. Elin had already made her comments on it, and Lars could only shake his head -

such a car cost as much as he earned in a year, or even more, and this youngster drove it as a matter of course.

Lars now tailed him all day long to find out what the kid was up to. With a normal job you could definitely not afford a luxury car like that. If a good opportunity arose, he would try to get into conversation with him, but that remained to be seen. He had until 6 PM, when Elin would replace him. He was to go to Lisa's tonight. She had sent him a text message asking if they could talk.

He had been surprised; he had wanted to ask her himself. Her hostility towards him was becoming more and more annoying, and he would definitely bring it up tonight. Now she had beaten him to it, and he wondered what it was all about. Was there anything new to complain about, something he had done wrong? Or did she want to change the times the children were with him? He would know soon enough. Stina had told him the other day that Lisa had been sad the last few days. Was there another problem? Or did she miss him? Well, she hadn't given him any reason to hope for it, and in order not to be disappointed, he preferred not to expect it.

Two hours later, shortly after 11 AM, this Mehmed finally came out of the building. He should have guessed that this guy was not an early riser. He went straight to his Cayenne and drove south on the E18 motorway. Lars followed him at a safe distance, because of the tracking device he didn't have to worry about losing Mehmed. Furthermore, the Cayenne was built higher than normal cars, so Lars always had him in his sights. Only if a truck or van was in the way, he switched to another lane in order not to lose visual contact.

Mehmed turned off at Rinkeby onto highway 279, then he drove on to the inner-city airport Bromma. In Stockholm there was much discussion whether this airfield was really necessary. The residents around were in favor of shutting it down, and many politicians, especially from the Greens, had also tried to push through an appropriate decision. There were conflicting opinions, and so everything was pretty ambiguous. Lars could understand that the airport was certainly not ideally located here from an environmental point of view. On the other hand, he was unable to judge how big the expansion potential of the large Arlanda airport was. Actually, there was a lot of space 25 miles north of Stockholm, there was nothing but forest and meadows all around. Sometimes he suspected that many frequent flyers simply found Bromma more practical, as it was more central, and you could park right next to the terminal. The check-in was also much faster, the machines were smaller as they flew mainly within Sweden.

Anyway, Mehmed obviously did not want to go to the airport but drove past it and then turned off to Bromma and finally to Abrahamsberg, where he parked his car in a side street. He disappeared in house number 7 in Montörvägen. Lars found a parking lot across the street. During the next two hours not much happened, a woman with shopping bags entered the house, and three men arrived, each of whom stopped in front of the house, made a short phone call and was then let in. The first one stayed for about an hour, the second only half an hour. Lars thought he recognized that it was Mehmed who opened the door. Shortly after the last man who stayed for only twenty minutes had left, Mehmed also came out. Once again, he started driving the car. At first Lars thought that Mehmed would drive back home, but he didn't take the E18 north, instead he took the direction of Kista, where he then turned north onto the E4. He drove almost 20 miles on the E4, then took an exit before Arlanda Airport, to Märsta. There he drove into the village and parked his car in a parking garage on Frejgatan. He bought a ticket and entered house number 59.

Here the same thing happened again; he remained for three hours, and three men of different ages arrived, whom Mehmed - as far as Lars could tell - met at the front door. One of the men spoke to Mehmed only briefly, then he went back to his car and drove away, apparently there had been no business for some reason. It was obvious what was going on. Mehmed seemed to have a girl selling sex in each of the two houses. The question was only whether they were adult prostitutes or whether Mehmed was also doing the loverboy thing and the girls were in a similar situation to Hanna. Unfortunately, Lars could not see which apartments were involved, and the girls did not appear anyway. But this could be found out by a targeted surveillance, Mehmed was obviously only with the girls by the hour.

Lars thought of the apartment in Botkyrka where Hanna had met her customers. Yesterday he had been there to inspect it, together with a cop and the lawyer. The apartment was a bit run-down, anything but nicely furnished, only the bedroom stood out - there were thick curtains, towels and red lighting. However, there were also personal things in the night cupboards, so it looked as if at least Hanna had lived in the apartment. Tulegatan was a great contrast to this, the furniture was solid and modern, the electrical appliances in the kitchen as well as the TV were up to date, and nothing suggested that clients had visited there. Everything pointed to the fact that Ali had used the Tulegatan apartment as his private residence, while the apartment in Botkyrka was used for business with Hanna. Apart from that, the crime scene hadn't revealed anything new, but Lars had taken a lot of photos of both apartments, so that they now had considerably more pictures than were available in the police report. In addition, the policeman had collected the broken glass and coffee cup fragments in plastic bags - they were to be examined for fingerprints. They would probably get the results early next week.

Mehmed left again around 5:30, and Lars followed him to his apartment in Jakobsberg. Shortly thereafter Elin replaced him, who arrived in a company car. Lars briefly told her how the day had gone and gave Elin the two addresses. Elin had had another meeting with Hanna today and, like the day before, had left out the subject of Ali – this way she had at least managed to hold the conversation in a pleasant atmosphere. Nevertheless, she was not satisfied, you could clearly see that. She wanted results that would help them make progress, her patience was already strained after three fruitless meetings. Tomorrow she might try to talk about the relationship with Ali. Lars wished her good luck and left Jakobsberg.

***

The drive over to Lisa's had gone fast. There was still a sting every time Lars parked the car in front of the house. How many times had he done that when returning home, looking forward to a relaxing evening? Now he was only visiting here.

The children opened the door and hugged him, both happy. Olivia took him by the hand and led him to the dining table. Lisa had made *köttbullar* with crushed potatoes and cranberries, the children chowed them down. Lars drank a light beer, Lisa went for water, even though she didn't have to drive anymore that evening. She had often had a glass of white wine with dinner. After dinner the children disappeared upstairs to their rooms, and Lars was left alone with Lisa. She got him another beer, she seemed nervous. She didn't look well at all, she had dark rings under her eyes and seemed to have her mind somewhere else. She had hardly participated in the conversations during the meal.

She sat down opposite him and looked at him. Something was wrong, Lars had a bad feeling about it.

"Lars ..." she began. He waited.

"I have something to tell you." She had slumped down on her chair, her chin shaking. It had to be something bad.

She looked up at him, her face was contorted in pain. "I have cancer," she finally blurted out, then collapsed over the table, put her head on her arms and cried.

Lars was thunderstruck, he hadn't expected that. All kinds of thoughts rushed through his head – would Lisa die? Did the children know about it? Why did she tell him that? He didn't quite know what to do now. In the past he would have taken her in his arms and comforted her, but since their separation Lisa didn't want any physical contact with him anymore. In the end, he found the courage to bend over and caress her upper arm. "I'm... I'm very sorry, Lisa," he said softly. "How bad is it?"

When she had calmed down a bit, she looked up and took his hand. He squeezed it. Lisa's make-up was smudged, her face was puffy. "Breast cancer. It's already advanced, they have to remove both breasts. followed by chemotherapy and radiation."

Lars was shocked, that didn't bode well. "How come? You're still so young." Lisa was three years younger than he was, she had just turned 37.

"I guess it runs in the family, my Aunt Pia had breast cancer at 35." Right, the younger sister of his mother-in-law, Lars could remember the funeral, which had been a year after they had married. He got chills up and down his spine.

"How did you notice that?"

"I felt a lump, so I went to the gynecologist, then to have a mammogram. Last week they did a biopsy, the results came back the day before yesterday. It is malignant and an aggressive form. You can't do anything with hormones either."

"Shit." Lars got up. "I'm so sorry, Lisa. I am completely shocked. I think I need something stronger now." He looked around for the whisky bottle that had usually been standing on the sideboard.

"Bottom of the cupboard, right-hand compartment."

Lars bent down and took out the bottle and two glasses. "Want some?"

Lisa shook her head. "No, I'm not drinking anymore. Just trying to live as healthy as possible. Whatever the hell good that does me now."

Lars took a seat on the chair next to her and poured himself a glass. He took a strong sip, which he needed now.

"But you will be okay, won't you?"

"There is a chance. But if the cancer has already spread, and doctors assume this because of the size of the tumors, then it's only a 20% chance."

"No. Oh, Lisa." Lars took another sip, his throat was burning, but it distracted him. He moved closer to her and put his hand on her shoulder. "You can do it, Lisa. You're young and strong."

She nodded boldly and swallowed.

"Where are you receiving treatment?"

"Karolinska."

"Do they know what they're doing?"

"Yes, I think so. The doctor caring for me is very nice, and there's a whole team treating me."

Lars looked at her, had she lost weight? She looked thin and fragile. That was not the Lisa he knew.

"What can I do, Lisa? I'll help you, whatever it is you need."

"Thank you." She looked at him sadly. "I'm going to need your help. Can you stay here with the kids while I'm at the hospital?"

"Sure. Of course, I will. How long will that be?" Lars liked being here, but it would mess up his feelings again. Anyway, it had to be done now. And it was the best solution, it was too cramped at his place, and the children had their school around the corner, so it was logical that he moved here.

"Probably for a couple of weeks, they want to do the first cycles of chemo as an IV, then maybe after that I could take tablets, in this case I could be at home, but I won't be fully up to speed."

"Don't worry about it. I'll move in here and stay as long as you want. I can take care of you when you get home. I still have some vacation time I can take."

"Thank you, Lars." She had tears in her eyes again. "I give you credit for that." She swallowed. "I wanted to tell you something else…"

Lars froze. What came next? Was there more bad news?

She took a deep breath. "You know, when you're in a situation like this, you start thinking about a lot of things."

Lars nodded; he could very well imagine that.

"I think I was pretty unfair to you. I tried to force you to do something you didn't want to do. And I'm sorry for that. It wasn't right."

Lars was flabbergasted. He would never have thought it possible that Lisa would ever come to this insight. He stared at her with big eyes.

"You don't have to say anything. I just wanted to get that out. I think it was wrong of me to force our separation that way. And I could understand if you didn't want to help me now. I don't exactly deserve it."

Lars didn't know what to say. He drank the rest of the whisky from the glass. He was touched.

Eventually he pulled himself together and said, "I'll help you, no matter what happens. You still mean a lot to me, and I still suffer from the fact that we're no longer a family."

"Oh, Lars." Lisa fell around his neck; he felt her wet face against his skin. He put down his glass and put his arms around her. What was that supposed to mean? Did Lisa want a fresh start? Or was it all because of her illness? Anyway, it was wonderful to hold her in his arms again. He would do what he could to help her through the treatment. He was more than happy to spend more time with the children again. They would have to see what would happen afterwards. The most important thing was that the treatment worked, and Lisa recovered.

31

Lars drove behind the Cayenne at a safe distance. He had mounted the iPad with the GPS software on the dashboard, the red dot was visible on the map two intersections in front of him.

He had relieved Elin at noontime, she had another appointment with Hanna that afternoon. She reported that nothing new had happened during the morning hours, Mehmed had been back in the apartment in Abrahamsberg and then had gone home. There Lars had taken over the supervision.

He had been preoccupied with something the entire time, but he hadn't been able to figure out what it was. Even this morning, when he had woken up, he had the feeling that he had missed an important detail. And yes, even yesterday he had a sudden thought flash through his mind as he had followed Mehmed for the first time. It seemed to have to do with Mehmed's luxury car, but no matter how much he racked his brain over it, he couldn't quite put his finger on the detail. Had he dreamt something? Or was there really a detail in his subconscious that he just couldn't bring to the surface?

He had slept at Lisa's last night, because after having several shots of whisky he hadn't been able to drive anymore. First, he wanted to sleep in the guest room, but Lisa preferred not to be alone. So one thing led to another, she sought his closeness, everything was so familiar, they were both emotionally upset. He was uncertain if it was the right thing to do, but it had happened - they had slept together. On the one hand there was that, on the other hand the news of Lisa's illness - it was not surprising that he was distracted and was missing out on something.

Today, Mehmed drove the same route as the day before. He went to Märsta, to the same parking garage, and he disappeared again in the same house. If nothing new came up soon, they could actually stop this surveillance, Mehmed seemed to be commuting back and forth between the three addresses.

Lars turned off the engine and prepared to wait a few hours. When he took out his cell phone, he saw that he had received an email from Edvard. He informed him that fingerprints were now being searched for on the broken glass at the crime scene. That was great. However, they couldn't read the navigation system from the Audi because the car had already been returned to its owner. Lars hesitated. Of course. He hit his forehead with the palm of his hand. That was the detail that had eluded him. The Audi had not been registered to Ali, he had found that out the very day he had tracked down Hanna and Ali. Only it hadn't been important anymore, because the case was closed. Therefore, it had not mattered who Ali's car belonged to. He scrolled feverishly through his text messages. Where was the inquiry to *Transportstyrelsen?* Yes, he had it there. The Audi RS5 was registered to a Najib Abadi. It was imperative that they included him in their research, as far as he knew, the name had never been mentioned before.

He sent a text message to Elin, asking her to investigate further. How could he have forgotten this detail? He could not understand it. This kind of thing had never happened to him before. Well, it was understandable that he was a bit confused since the conversation with Lisa, but that had been last night. He had received this text message months ago, and they had been working on this case again for two weeks. But he hadn't thought of this text message once.

In Frejgatan 59, the same game was going on as the day before. Twice customers arrived who were let in downstairs. Lars thought about intercepting one of them as he left the house and trying to find out something about Mehmed's girl. But he decided against it, after all it was a criminal offence to buy sex, and how could he explain to the john how he knew for what purpose he had been in the house. No, the men would play dumb and not say a word. There was even a risk that they would complain to Mehmed. If Mehmed knew someone was snooping around, he would be much more careful. So, he preferred to stick to observing for now. Mehmed stayed in this apartment all afternoon. This gave Lars time to think about Lisa and the future.

32

By now she already knew the procedure. Hand in your handbag, cell phone and everything from your pockets, then through the scanner and finally take off your shoes. The staff was not unfriendly, but still quite humorless. It was the fourth time that Elin visited Hanna. On the last two visits Hanna had at least talked to her, Elin had told her about a conversation with Klara, and that had interested Hanna a little. Elin had reported what was going on with Klara and how the class was doing. Hanna had first listened carefully and even begun to ask questions. In the end she wanted to know what was said about her at school. Elin couldn't answer that, but she had promised to ask Klara. This gave her a good kick-off for today's conversation. Elin was pleasantly surprised that Hanna was interested in this. Was that an indication of change?

The guard walked in front of her and unlocked the next door, there were a total of three that had to be passed before you came to the visiting rooms. At last Elin was let into the small room.

"It'll only take a few minutes, then she'll be here," said the guard. Had she smiled slightly? She turned around, her blond braid swung over her shoulder, then the door was closed. It was completely silent, Elin sat down on one of the two uncomfortable chairs at the small table. The room was boring as always, light green painted walls without pictures, on the floor a grey PVC foil. Elin had a plan for today, she wanted to try to talk to Hanna about Ali. Maja had given her an idea how she could do it. But it all depended on how the first part of the conversation went.

The door opened, the guard pushed Hanna into the room. She was wearing the same jogging suit as the previous times, black with red stripes. She kept her eyes lowered, was slumped over and just shuffled over to the chair on the other side of the table. She was pale and still looked miserable, no change from the last few days. The suit hung down her body as if it were two sizes too big.

"*Hej* Hanna." Elin smiled at her.

Hanna looked up briefly and nodded.

Elin leaned forward. "Say, I know you don't like the food here, but are you eating anything at all?"

"Yeah."

"But not much, right?"

Hanna shrugged her shoulders.

Elin waited, but nothing more came. She would draw Edvard's attention to it, but it was probably not worth pursuing the subject further here.

"We talked about your school yesterday, remember?"

Hanna looked at her with her grey eyes and nodded. She kept a straight face.

"You wanted to know what your classmates thought of you."

"Yes." She lowered her eyes again.

"That's why I spoke to Klara again." No response. "You want to know what she said?"

Another nod of the head.

"Well, you probably guessed that they were really bad-mouthing you, right? Like, what a whore..."

Now she had her attention, her head had shot up, Hanna stared at her, her mouth was slightly open.

Elin shook her head. "But that's not what is happening."

"What... what did she say?"

"Klara said she misses you. She'd like to see you." Elin wanted Hanna to ask questions. "Can she visit you?"

"I don't know." Hanna slid around on her chair, she bit one of her fingernails. "What does she think of me?"

Finally this question came up. "Do you mean Klara?"

Hanna nodded, still nibbling on her index finger.

"She thinks it was strong of you to run away from your parents. She admires you for living in your own apartment with Ali." That was the test, Elin had mentioned Ali. Would Hanna shut down now? Elin watched her closely, she saw Hanna flinch at the mention of the name. But she maintained eye contact, which was a good sign. Elin continued. "She said to tell you she's sorry."

Hanna frowned; she obviously did not know what Elin meant. "What?"

"What she's sorry for?"

Hanna nodded.

"That Ali is dead." The second time now the name had been mentioned, this time she did not flinch. But tears welled up in her eyes, her face distorted.

So Maja had been right. Last night they had talked about how Elin could get Hanna to talk about Ali. Maja was of the opinion that Hanna still loved Ali. She believed that these loverboys were really good and that the girls fell hopelessly for these guys, otherwise they wouldn't go on the streets for them. And those feelings couldn't be turned off so suddenly. "But they had a fight and Hanna probably killed him, albeit in self-defense," Elin had objected. Maja had shrugged her shoulders. "You weren't there, you don't know all that. And even if true, she could still love him. Talk positively about Ali, maybe she'll react." And she had been right about that, Hanna's reaction confirmed it.

"You love him deeply, don't you?"

Now Hanna collapsed, she put her arms on the table and cried uncontrollably. Elin leaned forward and stroked her shoulder. "I know, Hanna. It is terrible. You miss him more than anything."

Hanna grunted and cried even louder. Elin continued stroking her, finally she got up, went to the other side of the table and squatted next to her. She put her arm around her shoulders and said softly: "I'm so sorry, I'm sure you were very happy with him."

Hanna raised her head, her face was wet with tears, her hair hung wet over her cheeks.

"I want to be on the roof with him again, in his arms." Elin assumed that she was talking about the roof of the building in Tulegatan, which seemed to be a nice memory for her. Hanna looked at her with tortured eyes, then turned her upper body slightly towards Elin. Elin seized the opportunity and took the young girl in her arms. Hanna let her do so and laid her head on Elin's shoulder, she continued to cry softly and whispered something, Elin couldn't understand what she was saying. She gently stroked her head.

She really felt sorry for her, she was still a little girl, just 16 years old, who had been misled and suffered a lot. Elin didn't want to imagine what it was like to have sex with strangers, it really had to take a lot of self-overcoming. But Hanna's feelings for Ali were real, otherwise she wouldn't have done all this. And now this Ali was dead - the center of her life. She was all alone, she had isolated herself from everyone else. But how could Elin help her?

She held the thin girl in her arms and stroked her, she felt her breathing gradually slow down, and finally Hanna was completely silent. Elin waited a while longer. Then she asked quietly: "What can I do for you?"

Hanna whispered again, but this time Elin could understand her. "I don't know, but it's nice when you hold me like this."

Elin hugged her; she must have done something right. "I can hold you as long as you want."

She kept holding Hanna and waiting. Hanna was very quiet now; she didn't seem to cry anymore. Elin gathered up her courage. "You didn't kill him."

At first there was no reaction, but then Hanna shook her head slowly.

"Do you want to tell me what happened that day?"

"I don't know," she whispered.

"But you want us to find the one who did it, don't you?"

Hanna didn't respond. Elin waited.

Slowly Hanna began to speak, very quietly, Elin had to listen very carefully.

"I was so worried; he did not come home all night. And I couldn't reach him." Hanna swallowed; Elin continued to stroke her shoulder.

"Then I thought maybe he had gone to Tulegatan. That's why I went there. The key was in his night table. When I got there, at first, I thought that he wasn't there either. It smelled weird, but everything was quiet. Then I made myself a coffee and went into the living room. There he was." She sobbed and Elin held her close. "Ali was lying on the carpet next to the couch, I dropped the coffee cup in horror. He did not move, there was a big knife in his chest. I fell down, stepping on something slippery, almost slipped. It was horrible, there was blood everywhere. I shook him and kept screaming 'Ali, please! You can't be dead.' But he just stared expressionlessly into the air, there was no reaction. His skin was warm, though. I thought that I have to pull out this knife, maybe he will wake up again. But when I got it out, more blood came out of the wound and Ali didn't move. I was completely desperate and screamed for help. I cried on his shoulder until the police came. After that I don't know anything anymore."

Elin continued to hold her. "Good, Hanna. None of this was your fault. I knew it. It's good that you told me. I think you feel better now, right?"

Hanna nodded slowly. They sat like this for a while longer, tightly embraced, each in her own thoughts, until the guard opened the door and announced that time was up. Slowly and reluctantly Elin let go of the girl. She smiled encouragingly at Hanna. "Should I come back tomorrow?"

"Yes, please." Hanna slowly walked to the door, her face was swollen, but her shoulders were not hanging as low as when she came in. Elin felt like she had run a marathon, even though she didn't know how it felt because she had never run one before. It was as if she was completely worn out, all energy had vanished. She sat down on Hanna's chair and took a deep breath.

***

She worked feverishly on the PC. It was like she had been shot when she got out of Kungsholmen prison, but then she had seen the text message from Lars. She was electrified by the fact that Ali's Audi was not registered to Ali himself, but to someone else. That was clearly a new lead. She went straight to the office and checked out the name. She would never have thought that the Audi could not have belonged to Ali, nor had there been any reason to check that. She had only noticed the license plate number in the police report because she had never seen the car when she was looking for Hanna prior to the summer. Once Lars had found it, the case was closed within a few hours. They hadn't bothered with it anymore.

This Najib Abadi was definitely a special character. Either he was an extremely successful businessman, or he had come into his fortune by criminal means. Of course, Elin could not rule out an inheritance, but it was more likely to come from abroad, because the name was clearly not a Swedish one. Najib lived in a huge house on the northern edge of Södertälje, together with his wife Akasma. She was 32, he 48. Elin had found a picture of them on Facebook. Akasma had a page there and uploaded lots of photos. She was a pretty woman, heavily made up and in a sexy outfit. Big, brown eyes, curved lips and wavy dark hair down to her shoulders. Najib, on the other hand, had an unmistakable belly, wore a three-day beard and had a bald forehead. She didn't like the man; he had a look on his face that made it clear that he wasn't someone to cross.

Elin also gathered information about the cars they drove. While the wife had a Golf GTX, five cars were registered to Najib, of which Ali's Audi RS5 was the least expensive. Elin was quite astonished - there was an appropriate car for every purpose: a Mercedes S600 for moving around in comfort, an Aston Martin Vanquish for sporty driving, a Lamborghini Urus for the SUV fan and a Ford F-450 - that was such a monster pick-up, ideal for transporting something. Of course, she could not exclude that one of the other four cars was also lent to someone like Ali. But actually, she didn't believe that, the Audi RS5 seemed to be the only one that was still relatively normal compared to the others and at least one price range lower. The Audi was also the most recent purchase - registered in January of that year.

Najib was involved in half a dozen companies, all of them with meaningless names and broad descriptions of their field of activity. The largest company had a turnover in the high double-digit millions and ten employees. With a more intensive search, Elin finally found out that this company owned a nightclub, the *VIP Nightclub*. Interestingly, it was located in Enskede, on Rökerigatan, a stone's throw from the Globen. Ali had stayed somewhere in the vicinity on the morning of the day he died. It could be a coincidence, but Elin did not believe in coincidences. The nightclub would open tonight at ten, and Elin wanted to check it out.

Carl had also delivered, and it was quite obvious that Ali had visited this Najib several times, about every two weeks, but only for half an hour at a time. The owner of the phone number they believed belonged to this Mehmed, however, had been meeting Ali constantly, usually for several hours and almost every day. They had been together in Tulegatan, at Mehmed's address in Jakobsberg and again and again near the Globen. They had also visited numerous locations in Stockholm in the evenings, which Elin could match to bars or clubs. The area around the *VIP*

Nightclub also regularly turned up. In the nightclub itself, the signal from the telephones seemed to be quite well shielded, so that the location became inaccurate. However, both phones could be located on the street before entering and after leaving this nightclub. So, Elin assumed that the two had spent several hours in the club each time. All the more reason to go there.

Several times Elin tried to reach Lars, but his phone was always busy. She would have liked to inform him about the progress with Hanna and also about the results of her research on this Najib. She considered sending him a message, but she wanted to hear his reaction when she told him about the breakthrough with Hanna. Anyway, she would certainly be able to get in touch with him tomorrow, and then she could even report her observations at the nightclub.

33

This time they seemed to be going to a new destination, they had not driven from Märsta to Mehmed's apartment in Jakobsberg again, nor to his girl in Abrahamsberg, but had gone through Stockholm on the motorway via Essingeleden, and then continued their journey east on highway 75. Now Lars had moved a little closer to the Cayenne, they drove south on highway 73, and Mehmed turned right at the first roundabout, just as Lars was passing the Globen, one of Stockholm's landmarks. The Globen is the largest spherical building in the world and is used as an arena for sports and music events. Whenever Lars passed by here, he always had to think of the ice hockey games he had seen here when he was still attending school.

Mehmed drove to a residential area in Enskede. That was interesting. Was this a new address - did he have three girls? And Ali had also been around here somewhere before he went to Tulegatan that last time. While Lars slowly followed the route on the map, the red dot seemed to have reached its destination. He had to turn twice, then he saw the Cayenne in a parking space at the side of the road. Mehmed just crossed the road and disappeared in a two-story apartment building on the other side. He did not pay attention to Lars. Unfortunately, Mehmed had taken the only free parking space in Drivhusvägen, Lars had to drive down a side street to park his Volvo.

Elin absolutely had to cross-check this address with Ali's movement data. Lars looked at the clock, it was already after 6 PM, Elin would probably be home by now. She could carry out this task tomorrow, on Saturday. He would have preferred to go home earlier today to spend the evening with Lisa and the children, but that wouldn't be possible, he didn't want to miss Mehmed's evening program.

The children had been astonished in the morning when he had been sitting at the breakfast table. They were also very happy about it. Almost like before, the four of them together like a really happy family. If it hadn't been for the fact that Lisa was sick. She wanted to tell the children over the weekend, because on Monday she had to go to the hospital for the surgery. This meant that Lars had to pack his bag this weekend to go back to Hässelby to live with the children. Of course, he also had to talk to Elin and Tobias, because he would not be able to work during the evenings and weekends for the next few weeks since he had to take care of the children. And when Lisa would come home and continue the chemotherapy there, Lars wanted to take time off. He could only hope that they had finished this case by then.

He used the time he had to wait to talk to Lisa on the phone. She sounded quite different from usual, much friendlier. She also seemed relieved that she had been able to settle everything with Lars, both emotionally and logistically, so that she could now go to the clinic without worrying about the children. However, she still had to talk to the children, and it was obvious that she had the jitters about it. She wished that Lars was there when she told them. Of course, he agreed to it. He suggested to join them for breakfast the following morning. He didn't know what time it would be tonight. Lisa agreed immediately. Everything was much easier with her now. He wasn't sure if it would stay that way or if she was only being tolerant for now, because she was counting on his help. But he had the impression that the terrifying news of her illness had triggered a process of reflection in her. Once again, he thought that all they could hope for was a recovery of Lisa, so that they could really benefit from this change.

At the entrance to the house where Mehmed had disappeared, something happened. Mehmed had opened the door and was talking to an older man. It went back and forth for a while, then the man shook his head, turned around and left. It seemed that a deal had not been reached. Lars assumed that there was indeed another girl working for Mehmed. In the following three hours his assumption was confirmed, because two more men were met downstairs - and both times there seemed to be no problems, both men went with Mehmed without hesitation.

Lars had decided to stay here until Mehmed went back home, wanting to get a complete picture of his daily routine. Actually, he had assumed that Mehmed would go back to his apartment in Jakobsberg late in the evening. But everything came out differently.

After the second of the customers had left the house shortly after 10 PM, it took only fifteen minutes until Mehmed stepped out the front door, together with a girl. Lars just managed to get his smartphone in position to take some pictures, then the two of them disappeared around the next corner of the next house. The girl was quite dressed up – black leather miniskirt, a low-cut beige blouse and lots of costume jewelry around her neck and on her arms and on her feet were high-heeled black boots. The blonde hair was wavy and reached down over her shoulder. She was heavily made up, so her exact age was difficult to estimate. Because of her slim figure Lars nonetheless assumed that she was under 20. The two of them had not gone to the Cayenne, as he had first assumed, but seemed to be aiming at a target on foot. Lars thought about whether it would be better for him to follow by car or to run after them. He decided to get out of the car. He was afraid of attracting attention with his car if he slowly followed them, there was almost no traffic here at this time. He sprinted to the corner of the house and just saw the two of them disappearing hand in hand around the next corner. His decision had been right, because as he saw now, this street, the Planterarvägen, was a dead end, his Volvo would have been of no use to him. He made a short sprint, even though his knee was complaining, and followed the pair around the next corner. He had narrowed the gap, and that was a good thing, because the two were crossing through a residential area on narrow pedestrian paths. Here he could easily have lost sight of them. There were bushes everywhere, and it was dawning. Luckily neither of them turned around, apparently, they didn't suspect that anyone might follow them. After passing by a kindergarten, they left the residential area behind and ended up on Lindevägen - Lars knew the name because he had parked his car at the other end of this street. However, they turned in the opposite direction, passing a small wood on Trädskolevägen. Here the ground became clear again, it was only possible to go straight ahead, so Lars let himself fall back a bit. Except for himself and the two in front of him, there was nobody else around. In the street there was a car repair shop and a car rental, both of which were closed at this time. After that there was a gas station where several customers were just pumping gas. Here Lars accelerated his steps, because the couple crossed the street and entered the entrance to an industrial area right next to the Tele2-Arena. The arena was the home stadium of two soccer teams, Djurgården and Hammarby. But

Mehmed and his companion didn't want to go to the arena, they walked a bit into the industrial area. At the first opportunity they turned right, at a house made of red bricks with a high chimney. Lars stopped at the corner and watched them. There were hardly any pedestrians here, but lots of taxis dropping people off in the street. After a short wait, Lars followed the couple, he stayed on the other side of the street and tried to hide behind the taxis, which, considering his size, was only possible by ducking slightly. But he didn't have to walk for long, the couple had apparently reached their destination, they entered a nightclub, which was located in the basement of one of the houses. There was a line in the street, but Mehmed led the girl down the stairs and was immediately let in by the muscle-bound bouncer who was overseeing the entrance, without any kind of check. Since most clubs did not allow entry until the girl was 20 or even 21 years of age and strictly verified this, Lars assumed that Mehmed was known and well accepted here.

He sighed. He had no choice but to get in the line, because he would not be given special treatment. In front of him stood a group of young girls, probably about 25, all in party mood and dressed accordingly. They were chattering loudly to each other as the line slowly progressed. As was to be expected, the entrance was strictly regulated, everyone had to show their ID. Two young men were turned away, probably they were too young. One of them complained a little, but the bouncer had already moved on to the next person. By the way, he didn't look like someone you could argue with. It took more than ten minutes until it was Lars' turn. The doorman was a couple of inches shorter than him, but considerably broader. His head was clean-shaven, and in his left ear he wore a conspicuous hoop with a skull. He was dressed in black, with an emblem of the nightclub on his chest, and in his ear he had a black earphone. He carefully examined Lars, who already showed his identity card without being asked.

"Alone?"

"Yes, my girlfriend will be a little late," Lars lied.

The muscleman moved aside and nodded him in. That had been easy. Behind the dark red curtain there was another staircase, leading down to a lobby, where the coat room was located, but had little to do today since hardly anyone wore a jacket in the mild weather. Beyond the coat room were the bathrooms, and there were another three "sumo wrestlers" standing there, in the same clothes as the bouncer and also bald, apparently additional security personnel. On the other side of the room was a door marked "staff only", behind which the manager was probably sitting. The actual nightclub was located straight ahead. The music could already be heard softly on the street, but now it was getting really loud. It was a techno sound, which Lars did not like much, but he wasn't here for fun anyway. He roamed along the long bar, the other side of the room was a huge dance floor, but it wasn't very full yet. Nevertheless, the disco lighting was already in full swing, at the moment in blue and purple tones.

He was discreetly on the lookout for Mehmed and the girl but couldn't find them anywhere. They were not sitting at the bar, and they were not on the dance floor either. Lars sat down on a free bar stool and ordered a beer. He took a sip and turned to the dance floor. As he now noticed, there was another area behind it where you could sit on sofas at small tables. A lot of people were gathering there, maybe they were somewhere around there. Or perhaps they had gone through the tunnel at the end of the bar, which Lars hadn't noticed up to now. He got up to check first where this tunnel led to. Only when he had pushed himself through between the people standing around and rocking their glasses did he realize how huge this club was. You came into a second hall, again with a bar and lots of comfortable seating.

A third room followed, in which there was a second large dance floor. Modern pop was played here, and it was a bit busier than in the front rooms. Lars really had something to do if he wanted to find Mehmed here. He systematically roamed the various rooms and finally discovered the two in one of the sitting areas in the middle room. They sat alone and drank champagne from tall glasses. Lars found a couch not far from the two and put his glass down in front of him. He could watch the girl a little better now. He still didn't have the impression that she was an adult. Not that he was surprised, apparently Mehmed and Ali had the same taste or the same business model. After a while Lars took out his cell phone and saw that he had missed several calls from Elin. It was reasonably quiet here in this room, even if the music was streaming over from the adjacent rooms. He tried to call Elin, but found that he had no network at all, apparently the club down here in the basement was well shielded. He had been surprised that nobody was talking on the phone or surfing on his smartphone, now he knew why. Well, he would talk to Elin tomorrow, hoping that she had good news about her conversation with Hanna.

Lars watched Mehmed and his companion, but soon realised that Mehmed looked over at him a few times – had he noticed anything? When a group of three girls and two men joined the two – it could be concluded from the greeting that they knew each other well – Lars got up and strolled back to the bar. He ordered another beer and decided to wait here for a while. Mehmed or his girl could not leave this room without him being aware of it, the two exits were in view.

He was halfway through his beer and had just finished a short conversation with the bartender when someone sat down on the vacant stool next to him. Lars looked up and was surprised to find that it was Mehmed who had taken a seat here and was now ordering a drink – Red Bull with Jägermeister. Then he turned towards Lars. He had a broad face with a small scar under his lip. His brown eyes examined Lars.

"First time here?"

Lars nodded. "Is it that obvious?"

"It's a feeling you develop over time..."

"Oh, I see. So, you're here all the time?"

"Yep, several times a week." Mehmed took his drink. "What are you here for? Girls? I saw you looking at my chick."

Lars swallowed, the guy was attentive and quite direct. "Yeah, sorry, hope you're not mad."

"*Hej*, man, no issue. Do you like her?"

"She's cute, no arguing that."

"I can arrange a round with her." Mehmed sipped his drink and looked at him sharply over the glass.

So that's how it went. Lars played dumb. "I thought she was your girlfriend?"

Mehmed laughed. "One doesn't exclude the other, does it? You just have to pay a little bit."

That was obvious. "How much?"

"Depends on how long you want. 2,500 for an hour."

"That's a lot." Lars acted surprised.

"Dude, she's worth the money, believe me. And still really young. If you're quick enough, half an hour might be enough for you. It only costs 1,500."

"Is she of legal age yet?"

Mehmed winked. "Depends who's asking."

"Gotcha." Lars took a sip of his beer. "And where? Here at the club?"

"There's this quiet back room, very discreet."

Lars wondered – should he ask Mehmed about Ali now or would it be better to play the john and see if he got something out of the girl? Both had their risks. In the first case, Mehmed might shut down completely, and then he couldn't get to the girl either. In the second case it was quite possible that the teenager didn't know anything or wouldn't say anything. But then he would still have a second chance with Mehmed.

"Well, what? Do you want to?" Mehmed poked him in the elbow.

"I'd like to, but there's someone else I want to meet…"

Mehmed got up. "Don't think too long, dude – there are other people interested…" With that he turned around and went back to his table. For some reason, he had given up quickly. Was he gambling on Lars running after him? He drank his beer. Now what? Had he missed his chance? No, he could always sit with them and continue the conversation. He decided to wait a little longer, he did not want to appear too eager.

But it didn't come to that, suddenly someone snuggled up against him from behind and put her slender arm around him. "Hi, cutie." It was Mehmed's companion. She smiled seductively at him with her dark red painted lips. "Heard that you like me. Is it true?"

She smelled of a heavy perfume, her light blue eyes really stood out under the eye shadow and mascara. She stroked him tenderly on the neck, her fingers were very soft. The little chick clearly understood her job.

Lars had no choice. Not because he couldn't resist the blonde - he had no intention of having sex with her under any circumstances - but because if he refused, he would probably have a hard time getting close to Mehmed again, certainly not tonight.

"Okay, half an hour."

She blew him a kiss. "Well, I knew it. Come on, honey, let's have some fun." She took his hand and pulled him from his stool. With a wink, she turned around and dragged him behind her. Even on her high heels she was at least two heads shorter than him and very petite, her little butt dancing in front of him. She maneuvered him through the room with the techno beat, past the dressing room to the staff door. There she knocked three times, whereupon the door opened. Another bouncer, also the size of a refrigerator, or rather the size of a fridge-freezer combination. He nodded and let her pass. The little girl continued past several locked doors to the end of the hallway, where there was a door with a red heart. Behind it was a small room with reddish lights and a large bed with lots of pillows on it. The girl locked the door from inside and looked at him expectantly from below. She held out her hand.

Lars took out his wallet and counted three 500 bills, which the little girl immediately took. Then she let herself fall onto the bed, her beige blouse stretched over her breasts, which were apparently not held down by any bra. "What would you like, sweetie?"

Lars sat next to her. "I wanted to talk a little."

The little girl leaned on her back, her blonde curls bouncing. "What, talk? That's not what you paid for."

"I know. But if I get the right information, I'll throw in another brown bill. Without us having sex."

She tilted her head and looked at him suspiciously. "What kind of information? What are you, a cop?"

She really had a cute face, narrow, full lips, big eyes – Lars could imagine that it was not difficult for her to find customers. "No, I'm not with the police. By the way, you look very pretty."

The girl smiled at him. Lars thought she started trusting him and ventured further. "Do you know Ali?"

Her big eyes closed; her face turned away. "He's dead," she said in a deep voice.

"Exactly. He was a good friend of mine, and I'd like to know why he had to die. It just won't allow me any peace. Was he in trouble?"

She looked at him again, lips pressed together defiantly. "With Mehmed? They were great buddies."

"Maybe with someone else?"

"I don't know. You'll have to ask Mehmed."

Well, he wasn't getting anywhere here. "How many girls did Ali have?"

"You mean the likes of me?"

Lars nodded and looked at her expectantly.

"This is the first time he's ever done this. Just the one, this little gray mouse."

"Who helped him do it?"

She looked at the door, then she said, "First the 500."

Lars gave her the bill, which she stuffed into her skirt. "Well?"

"The boss."

"Who is that?"

She whispered. "Najib, he owns this place."

He knew the name. "I see. How did he help Ali?"

"With everything. He couldn't have done anything by himself."

"Give me some examples."

"The car, the apartment, all that kind of stuff."

"And were there any problems because of that?"

She shook her head. "You know, I think that's enough."

"Well, for 500, that wasn't much information."

"Your problem. We could have had sex." She looked at him defiantly.

"It's okay." Lars got up.

The girl looked at her watch. "It's only been ten minutes, so we'd better wait a little longer. Want me to give you a blowjob?"

Lars shook his head. "No, forget about it." But she was right, it would probably attract attention if they came back too soon.

"I'll speak to Mehmed again."

The girl opened her eyes. "What? But don't tell him I was talking to you, he'll beat me to a pulp." She looked at him pleadingly.

Lars nodded. "Okay, this is between you and me. We'll say that you gave me a blowjob and it went pretty fast. I was very pleased. Agreed?"

"Thank you." She lay down on the bed and took out her cell phone.

Lars checked his - oh, here he had a signal and Elin had tried to reach him again. However, he did not want to call Elin in the presence of the girl. Instead, he opened the new app that Tobias had bought for all the agency's employees. With it you could start a recording function. The trick was that the recording activity wasn't displayed anywhere, and the recording was streamed to the cloud in real time. Everything that was in the cloud could only be deleted by Tobias. This way, even if you got caught, you could still preserve evidence. Lars thought it would be useful to record a possible following conversation with Mehmed. Actually, it would have probably been even better to record the little ones' info already, but it all came about so quickly and unexpectedly that he hadn't even thought about it.

Ten minutes later, they left the room and went back to the bar. The girl leaned against him and whispered: "Don't forget what you promised me." Then she walked back to her table, where Mehmed welcomed her with a kiss on the cheek. Lars ordered another beer, this time without alcohol, after all he still had to drive. As he was about to pick up the glass, Mehmed appeared beside him.

"Well, old man, happy with my baby doll?"

Lars took a sip and grinned. "Absolutely, that girl is great."

"You're welcome again, man. Here's her number." He put a business card next to the beer coaster, on it was a woman in a provocative position, next to it the name "Lola" and a telephone number.

"Thank you." Lars put the card in his pocket. "Can I ask you something else?" It was now or never.

"Sure, man. What do you want to know?"

"You're a friend of Ali's, right?"

The friendly face disappeared at once; he became serious. "Why? Did you do business with him?"

"No, but I want to know why he was killed."

"Are you a cop?"

"No, I work for Hanna's lawyer." There was no point in saying otherwise now. "You don't believe Hanna killed him, do you? Ali must have had problems with someone else."

Lars watched him sharply, but he couldn't see any reaction, Mehmed kept his poker face.

"Not with me, dude."

"Then with whom?"

"Dude, watch your mouth," he hissed. "You're walking on thin ice." Then he turned around and went to the exit. Shit, just as he feared, the guy shut down. That was probably it. He could go home now. So he would call Elin when he was on the street, maybe she had news about Hanna. He drank the rest of his beer and got up. Just in this instant he felt a big hand on his shoulder. One of the sumo wrestlers.

"You be a good fellow and come with me." He turned Lars towards the exit and pushed him forward. That was quick, the communication in the club seemed to function smoothly. But he wanted to leave anyway, so it didn't matter that they threw him out. He did not resist and let the meatball guide him.

But he was wrong, because at the coat room, the Neanderthal didn't push him up the stairs, but instead into the personnel area. Suddenly there was a second guy next to him, each of them had one of his arms in a firm grip, and Lars had no chance to defend himself. They took him to one of the other doors, through which he was roughly pushed in. He almost fell to the ground, but just barely managed to catch himself in front of a large desk. Behind it sat a somewhat plump man with a high forehead and dark stubble.

The door was slammed shut behind him, he was pushed onto a chair, his arms pulled back. One of the two Neanderthals took out a roll of silver tape.

"Hey, what are you doing?", Lars complained, but that earned him nothing but a resounding slap in the face. Then his hands were tied behind the chair and taped to the backrest. His legs were also taped. One of the two giants searched his pockets - his cell phone, his wallet and his briefcase including car keys were placed on the desk. The fat man looked through everything.

"What do you want from me?" Lars slowly started to worry; the whole thing did not look good.

He got slapped again. "You speak when you are asked," grunted the Neanderthal on his right.

Lars decided to wait and see.

The fat man held up the cell phone. "Unlock it." He had a rasping voice.

The left Neanderthal man picked up the device and held the home button on Lars' right index finger. That was the disadvantage of this kind of identification, the fingerprint was super convenient, but in this situation not to his advantage, with a code this would not have happened.

The fat man scrolled through the cell phone; Lars could only hope that the recording function was really not recognizable. Apparently, the man was satisfied, he dropped the cell phone on the table and looked at Lars.

"Let's talk a bit. You are obviously very keen on it."

Lars waited, he still did not understand what was going on here. Such treatment just because he asked about Ali? He just wanted to get out of here.

"Private eye, eh?"

Lars nodded.

"Why are you interested in Ali?"

Lars saw no reason to hold back with his mission. "I have been hired by the suspected girl's defense attorney to look into the background of Ali's death. We do not believe the girl killed him."

The man stared at him with his piercing dark eyes. "Why do you think that?"

Good question. After all, it was only a hypothesis, they had no conclusive proof. But if he wanted to find out anything here, he'd have to put something on the table. So he decided to bluff – a decision he would regret.

"The girl's statement. And there is also evidence of at least one other person at the scene."

The fat man stared at him. He didn't seem to like the answer. He turned to the left Neanderthal.

"Get Mehmed."

Immediately the guard left the room, only to return within a few seconds. Lars turned to the door, Mehmed stood in the opening.

"Boss?"

"What did your bitch say?"

"She says he asked questions about Ali, but she just told him that we were buddies. She does not know anything anyway."

The fat man scratched his chin. "You get this guy out of here. Mehmed, go get your car."

"But... I have it at home."

"I don't care. You're the reason we have this problem, you're taking your car. Just hurry up."

Mehmed went and closed the door behind him.

"Get him out of here. He can wait somewhere else until Mehmed comes. Take the chair and make sure he keeps his mouth shut."

Lars was getting queasy, what were they up to? "Well, wait a minute, what's this all about? I didn't do any damage, just asked a few questions. I demand that you release me, and I'll leave immediately."

The boss nodded to the Neanderthal on the left and pointed to Lars. The man tore off a strip of the silver tape and stuck it over Lars' mouth. Then the two musclemen lifted him up with his chair and carried him out into the hallway and from there into an adjoining room. This seemed to be a kind of lounge for the staff, on the table were ashtrays and empty bottles. On one of the chairs sat Lola, with smudged make-up and a torn blouse. When the two guys had put Lars down, she stood up and punched him in the face with her flat hand. Compared to the slaps from the Neanderthal, however, this was more of a caress.

"You motherfucker. Do you know how much trouble you got me in?"

Lars couldn't reply because of the tape, but it didn't look like she expected an answer anyway, she left the room, together with the two giants. Lars was annoyed with himself; he had been too naive and had acted too directly. He had hoped to find out something here quickly so he could close the case and concentrate on Lisa. He thought about what would happen now. Apparently, they were going to take him away. Drop him off in the middle of nowhere and beat the crap out of him as a goodbye? That was the most likely scenario, and it wasn't much fun. It wouldn't be the first time he got a beating, but with no way to fight back, it wasn't exactly fun. He also wondered how Lisa would react if he came home with injuries now of all times. He tugged at his cuffs, but there was no room to maneuver and the silver tape was unfortunately extremely strong. Lars let his eyes wander through the room. Was there anything here he could free himself with? Yes, there was a bread knife on the back of the sink. If he stood on his feet and balanced the chair he was tied to, then he should be able to push himself there slowly. And if he could grab the knife, he might be able to cut the tape. He was about to lean forward when the door opened, and the Neanderthal came back. He sat down at the table, with a view of Lars. Shit, now he didn't stand a chance. All he could do now was to wait and see, given the surveillance.

Lars thought about his cell phone, which was now on the table with this fat guy. Probably it was that Najib, the way he was acting, he must be the boss here. As long as he didn't turn off the phone, it would record everything and send it to the cloud, maybe there would be something usable there. Reception was available in this area of the nightclub, so it was no problem. However, it was the first time Lars had really used this feature, he had only done a small test once before. Everything had worked out fine, but as it was with technology, when you really needed it, there were often problems. Anyway, he didn't have access to his phone and could only hope that the recording worked, and the guy said something that helped them before he switched off the device or the battery died.

***

Lars started to suffer from his uncomfortable position on the chair. Slowly his arms fell asleep. He tried to tense the muscles to get the blood flow going again. But that didn't really help, as soon as he stopped, the tingling sensation returned.

Finally, the second refrigerator reappeared, and they released him from the chair, but his hands remained tied. They put him on his legs, and one of them threw a jacket over his shoulders.

"You wanted to go, didn't you? We're going to help you get out of here. So come along quietly."

Lars made a sound of agreement under the tape, what else could he do?

They led him into the hallway, then through the door to the nightclub lobby. One of them was close in front of him, probably to shield him so you couldn't see his gag, the other grabbed him by his left arm and shoved him forward. They went up the stairs to the outside. There was a car right in front of the entrance that he knew well - a black Cayenne with red leather seats. They pushed him into the back seat, the guy on his arm followed and sat down beside him. Mehmed climbed in the front and immediately stepped on the gas.

A longer drive followed, how long Lars could not estimate, but at any rate, it wasn't just to the next corner to throw him out of there, as he had hoped. The Neanderthal had put the jacket over his head so he couldn't see where they were going. His arms were completely numb, he couldn't feel them anymore; they pressed into his back and made sitting anything but comfortable. He couldn't complain because the tape over his mouth prevented him from making anything other than grunts. He concentrated on breathing slowly and regularly through his nose. But the longer it took, the worse his condition became, every movement of the car hurt his shoulders. He also knew that this transport over a long distance was not good. They would beat him up at the minimum and leave him lying somewhere, and in the worst-case scenario, they wanted to eliminate him. He just did not understand why. He hadn't found out anything at all. But it must have meant that there was something to find out. These guys were dirty and now they reacted extremely sensitively just because he had shown up and asked a few questions.

After they made a few turns, the car sped up. Had they already left town? Then again, they slowed down and turned. Now it went slower, there were curves and crossings, Lars' shoulder was put under a lot of strain. The tire sounds became louder, the car shook harder, they were probably driving on some kind of dirt road. Lars had a chill running down his spine. Eventually the car came to a stop, the door was opened, and the Neanderthal tore Lars from his seat. He still had the jacket over his head. The engine of the Cayenne howled, and the car drove on. Lars took a punch right in the middle of the solar plexus, knocking the air out of him. The guy pushed him back a few steps and gave him a punch in the nose, and unfortunately the jacket did not cushion the blow at all. Lars had the feeling that his face exploded, something cracked, and blood flowed over his lips. He staggered backwards, but suddenly there was no more ground, he fell backwards into emptiness. Before he could think of anything, he hit a hard, sloping surface, so he kept falling, spinning around his own axis. Sharp pebbles penetrated his clothing, the speed of his rolling increased, he lost the jacket and could finally see what was happening. But now his face was no longer protected, sand and stones pressed themselves into his forehead and eyes. He rolled down a steep slope, and no matter how hard he tried, he could not slow down the descent. When he hit the ground with a thud, he lost consciousness.

When the tape over his mouth was torn off, Lars regained consciousness. Mehmed and the Neanderthal stood over him, they had sat him up and leaned his back against a rock. Around them seemed to be some kind of gravel pit or quarry. He took a deep breath, everything hurt him. The fucking tape had survived the fall and he still couldn't feel his arms. He was spitting up blood.

Mehmed crouched in front of him, he had a knife in his hand. "So now, you're going to tell us a little bit more. What do you know about Ali's death?"

Lars spat once more, the blood still ran from her nose, it was certainly broken. He gasped.

"Nothing. That's why I was asking you."

Mehmed gave the giant a signal, whereupon he kicked Lars strongly in the side with his boot. Lars writhed in pain and cried out loudly.

"Dude, you can make it easy or hard for yourself. Your choice."

Mehmed pulled him back up. "Again. What do you know about Ali?"

What could he tell them? Something they wanted to hear? "I know that he forced Hanna into prostitution. But she didn't kill him."

Mehmed held the knife to his throat. "There you go. Who did it then?"

Lars swallowed, the blade scratched his skin. "I think it was you."

"Do you have proof of this?"

"Not yet."

Mehmed nodded. "What do you know about the stuff?"

Lars stared at him. Was this about drugs? "What kind of dope? Only small amounts were found at Ali's place. I know nothing about that."

Mehmed looked at the Neanderthal. "Do we believe him?" The big guy shrugged his shoulders.

Mehmed got up. He folded up the knife and put it in his pocket. "Okay, let's finish him off."

The Neanderthal pulled Lars up, only to give him a hard hook in the chin right away. Lars went down, everything went black.

This could be a fun evening. Elin always liked it when you could combine work with pleasure. So, she was happy that Maja had agreed to accompany her to the club. They hadn't been dancing for a long time, Maja usually had to give lessons in the evening and afterwards she didn't feel like doing much of anything. But since Elin had to go to the club tonight anyway and had asked Maja for support, she had agreed. This was doubly good, because first of all it gave Elin security in case she ran into problems while snooping around - Maja was almost one head taller than Elin, strongly built, in great shape due to her work and of course a fantastic fighter. Secondly, they could have a lot of fun together.

Maja didn't come home until nine o'clock, they had eaten together, and Elin had told her about her success with Hanna. Afterwards they dressed up and finally it was almost midnight when they left - a good time for a nightclub visit.

They took the subway to Globen Station. From there, all they had to do was cross Palmfeltsvägen, and they could turn into Rökerigatan. Cars were not allowed to enter; flowerpots of concrete blocked the road - apparently, they had to come by car from the other side. From the train station you could still see the upper part of the Globen, but here in Rökerigatan the houses on both sides were quite high. They had to walk a long way down the street before they arrived at the *VIP Nightclub*. They walked arm in arm and were in a good mood. Maja wore her long dark hair loose, which she didn't do often. Her dark red blouse was a great contrast.

Elin had just spotted the entrance to the club on the opposite side - there was a purple neon sign above it – when a dark car approached them, at quite a high speed for this little road. She turned around as the car rushed by.

"I don't believe it. That's this Mehmed's car." Elin had recognized the license plate.

"You mean the guy you were surveilling today?"

"Exactly." Elin watched as the car behind them turned into the next side street, backed up and turned around. The Cayenne passed them again and stopped right in front of the nightclub, on the wrong side of the street. A taxi honked, it came from the opposite direction and had trouble getting past. But the driver of the Cayenne didn't seem to care.

"Come on, let's go over. I want to see if it's Mehmed who's in there."

They crossed the road behind the Porsche and passed the car. The back of the car was not visible, the windows were too heavily tinted. Nobody was sitting in front, the driver must have got out of the car immediately after stopping, the engine was still running. Elin looked around but couldn't see Mehmed anywhere. He probably had disappeared into the nightclub, but everyone else had to wait, as you could tell by the bunch of young people in front of the entrance. Two bouncers in black and with little buttons in their ears stood in front of the stairs leading down to the club and controlled the entrance. Elin pulled Maja forward and they positioned themselves at the end of the line – from here Elin had a good view of both the Cayenne and the entrance of the club without attracting attention herself. She was curious if it was really Mehmed who was driving the car and who Mehmed was picking up here. Maybe one of his girls? She had her cell phone ready to take some snapshots. It didn't take long, and a big guy came up the stairs, closely followed by two other big men. The second one walked a little bent over and was pushed forward brutally by the last one. Elin took a photo, and then her jaw dropped in shock. Fucking hell, that was Lars.

The first giant tore open the back door, Lars was pushed in, the last man sat down next to him. Then the giant slammed the door. At that moment Mehmed rushed up the stairs, threw himself into the driver's seat of the Porsche and stepped on the gas. Elin was so stunned that she forgot to take more photos.

"Hey, he looked like Lars." Maja tugged her sleeve.

Elin turned to Maja. "Shit, Maja, that was Lars," she hissed softly. She looked at the entrance. The giant was talking to the doorman, both were dressed in the same black clothes, they both had to be security guards. Why had they put Lars in the car with Mehmed?

"He was tied up."

"What?" Elin hadn't even noticed. She opened the picture she had just taken and enlarged the section of Lars. He wore a jacket over his shoulders, but it was too short to cover his hands, which protruded below - his hands were tied behind his back. What was going on here?

"We must go after him," Elin said. "We need a taxi."

"Over there." Maja pointed in the direction from which they had come. Elin sprinted off, the taxi sign was lit, so it was free. Maja followed, they tore open the back doors and threw themselves onto the seats. The man turned to them. He looked like maybe he was from India, with dark skin, jet-black hair and a mustache.

"Quick, follow that Cayenne up ahead." Elin pointed to the front, the car was already far away, but the rear lights were just visible.

Maja leaned forward. "Hopefully we won't lose him, he's going really fast."

"Hold on." Elin had just thought of something. After all, they had given the car a tracking device, and the app was also installed on her smartphone. She logged in, went to the menu, selected Mehmed's car and - tada, there it was. Mehmed just drove past the Tele2 Arena.

"Okay, slowly", she said to the driver. "You don't have to drive so close; I can direct you."

She showed Maja the display. "Here, the red dot, that's it. We are here." She pointed to the blue dot.

"Oh, how convenient."

Elin nodded. Luckily, she had the app. "What do you think is going on?"

"It didn't look good. They forced Lars into the car."

"Yes, and the thing about the restraints makes the whole situation worse. I tried to reach Lars several times today, I thought he was sitting comfortably at home and turned the phone down. Instead he was probably snooping around in the nightclub and got caught." She wondered, she hadn't really told Lars anything about the club - had he searched for Najib on the internet himself and had come to the same results as she had? Or maybe he had followed Mehmed, but that guy had just arrived, hadn't he?

She gave instructions to the taxi driver; the Porsche had now turned onto highway 73 and was heading south. "Should we call the police?" she asked Maja.

Maja frowned. "I don't know. Maybe they'll drop Lars off at some corner and then drive back. Then we've spooked the horses for nothing. Besides, what are you going to tell them where they should go?"

"Well, we can say we're chasing a car that's carrying a colleague of mine, and where the car is headed."

"And you think they'll set up a roadblock and send three Black Marias to chase them?"

"I guess not." Maja was right, as she knew the Swedish police, they had to come up with some more facts before they started the engines.

Elin looked at her phone, still on 73. "I know another solution - I'll call Tobias." She rummaged in her handbag for her earphones, she wanted to keep an eye on the map with the points while she talked to Tobias. The phone showed zero ten, he would be happy. It rang.

"Elin? Do you know what time it is?", Tobias rumbled.

"Yes, but it's an emergency. Lars has been kidnapped. We're following him in a taxi."

"How? Shit. What hornet's nest have you stirred up again?"

"I can't explain it all to you now. But he was in the *VIP Nighclub* on Rökerigatan, and there two men tied him up and put him in a car, which we are now following. We have been watching the car for the last few days, so it has one of our trackers. You can follow it on the app. If I don't check in regularly or send you a distress signal, please call the police and send them to the location of that car." She gave him the tag and the number, then she hung up before Tobias could ask more questions. Phew, at least she was covered.

In the meantime, they had arrived in a small village called Länna, where Mehmed turned west to Lissma. When he arrived in Lissma, he took the 259 in a north-western direction. Here there were only woods and meadows.

Elin looked at Maja. "Do you still think that they just want to drop Lars off somewhere?"

Maja made a worried face. "If so, he will be glad that we will pick him up right away, because we're out in the middle of nowhere here. But to be honest, I have a bad feeling."

Elin nodded. Yes, this didn't look good. Either they wanted to finish him off for good, or he was to be held captive somewhere for longer. Maybe in a small forest hut somewhere out here.

They both looked at the map on the mobile phone display. The red dot was about a mile ahead, so the car was out of sight.

"He's turning off," Maja said.

Sure enough, the car turned left at the intersection in front of them, there was a small housing estate in the forest. However, Mehmed made another turn in front of it, towards the south, and there were no more houses there, only forest, an industrial area and even further south - a gravel pit.

"Do you see that?" Elin pointed to the gravel pit.

Maja nodded. "Tobias?"

"Yes, I'll let him know. But it'll probably be a while before anyone gets here."

Elin sent a text message to Tobias. "It leads into a gravel pit; I'm afraid Lars is in serious danger. Call the police."

The taxi driver seemed to get nervous and turned back. "Dangerous?"

"Yes, but not for you. You have to take a left up there and then immediately left again." The driver looked skeptical but turned forward again and blinked his lights.

Elin guided the taxi driver through the industrial area. In her app she could see that Mehmed's Porsche had stopped – in the middle of the gravel pit. When the taxi arrived at the entrance, the taxi driver refused to continue.

"No way, I'm not going in there." He stopped in front of the entrance. The gravel pit was surrounded by a high lattice fence, but the gate was wide open.

"Okay, then you stay here and wait for us." Elin took a photo of his license, which was attached to the dashboard. "If you don't wait, you'll get into real trouble. We leave our bags here."

Elin rummaged in her bag. Yes, there it was. "I brought my pepper spray. Nothing else, unfortunately. And you?"

Maja was also looking. She shook her head.

They got out and immediately fell into a light sprint. Elin had her cell phone with the card in one hand and her spray in the other.

Maja cursed. "These are clearly the wrong clothes." She was wearing nylon stockings and a short denim skirt, Elin had chosen tight trousers, but made of an elastic material. At least they both wore sneakers; they were actually dressed for dancing.

The sandy path went on for several hundred feet between trees; they jogged at a brisk but steady pace. Finally, they came to the actual gravel pit, the path made a bend to the right, in front of them was a blue-yellow curve sign, because behind it there was a steep slope. They carefully approached the edge and looked down. Down there, mountains of gravel and stones piled up, a labyrinth of paths led through in between.

"There they are." Maja pointed a bit further into the pit. There the Cayenne stood; the headlights were on. The men were nowhere in sight.

"Come on, let's walk a little further down this path. It must lead down into the pit at some point." Elin set herself in motion again. After about 500 feet they came to a crossroads, to the left it went downhill, where the Cayenne stood, with its back to them. Elin raised her hand.

"Quiet now," she whispered.

Slowly they crept down the path. It was dark, the only light source here were the headlights of the Cayenne. Elin and Maja were dressed in rather dark colors, so you wouldn't see them as long as they didn't make a sound. Elin peered desperately into the pit - where was Lars?

Only when they were halfway down the path could they see the men. They were in the light of the wagon, but a mountain of sand had obstructed their view earlier. Lars sat leaning against a rock, Mehmed crouched in front of him, the giant stood beside him. They talked, but their words couldn't be made out. Suddenly the giant swung out and kicked Lars. Lars' scream echoed through the gravel pit.

"Shit," cursed Elin. "We have to help him."

They stalked hurriedly but quietly towards the Cayenne. As they passed it, they saw the giant punch Lars with his fist. Lars fell down and did not move. Mehmed moved away from them and went to a large metal container with a conveyor belt attached at the front. He opened the small door to a switch box and pressed a few buttons, whereupon something in this container was set in motion, it sounded like a big roller. The conveyor belt started to move. The giant had grabbed Lars by the shoulder and dragged him to the belt.

"What the fuck are they up to?" Maja stared incredulously at the men.

Elin put her phone away. "They will throw him in there if we do not stop it. Let's go." She ran towards the giant. Maja followed her.

The giant only noticed her when she was just a few feet away from him. Immediately he let go of Lars who fell down lying unconscious. He shouted something that Elin didn't understand. She ran straight towards him, but only now realized what a closet the guy really was. It seemed to her as if he was almost a foot and a half taller than she was, and his muscle mass had to be at least twice as much as hers. She reached up her arm as high as she could and pressed the spray button. The giant cried out and pressed his arm in front of his face, she seemed to have hit her target nicely. But at that moment Mehmed appeared and rammed her from the side. Elin went down and rolled around her own axis a few times. Dazed, she straightened up and looked back: Maja and Mehmed wrestled with each other while the giant was still rubbing his face. Elin shook her head to clear her mind. She saw Maja kick Mehmed's knee, who screamed and buckled. Maja reacted with a hand kick against Mehmed's neck and he was already lying on the ground. But the giant had apparently recovered enough for him to intervene again - probably Elin hadn't hit him in the eyes as precisely as she had wanted. He put his strong arm around Maya's neck from behind and lifted her into the air. Maja floundered with her legs and tried to hit the giant's stomach with her elbows, but he only squeezed harder. Elin saw her face turn red. She was just about to take a run-up to attack the giant and somehow free Maja when a second car pulled up next to the Cayenne, the headlights were set to high beam and blinded them all. Was that the police already? But there was no blue light. Or was it backup for the gangsters? If so, they were screwed.

A door opened; a shot rang out. "Let's all put our hands up in the air, and freeze."

A deep voice that Elin did not recognize immediately. The giant let go of Maja and raised his hands. Maja got down on her knees and gasped, she rubbed her neck. Mehmed had sat up and also held his arms up.

"Tobias?", Elin stammered.

"Yes. I left as soon as you called. The police always take too long." Tobias lived in Nacka, it was a stone's throw to *Globen*, no wonder he had caught up with them so quickly. "Here, I brought zip ties with me. Tie them both up."

Elin narrowed her eyes and walked towards the bright light. Tobias leaned on the driver's door, his pistol at the ready. With his other hand he handed her a bundle of plastic strips. Elin took them to Maja, who had just pulled herself together.

"Are you okay?"

She nodded. "All good," she gagged out hoarsely.

Together they first bound Mehmed, then the giant. Tobias had come closer and held them both in check. They ziptied their hands behind their backs and then bound their ankles together as well. Then they turned their attention to Lars - he looked bad: His face was covered in blood, wounds everywhere, his clothes were dusty and torn. He was still unconscious; the blow must have hit him hard. Elin turned him on his side and tried to free him of his bonds.

"Do you have a knife?" she asked Tobias.

"Sure do. I have all the gear with me." He pointed to his belt, which had a knife sheath hanging from it.

"I'm glad you came. Thanks."

Tobias shrugged. "Can't let my best employees down."

That was probably the first praise she had ever heard come out of his mouth. It felt good. "Didn't know you had a gun."

"For a long time. Licensed and everything."

Elin pulled the knife out of its sheath and cut the tape. Lars' hands were just as badly damaged as his face.

"We need an ambulance for him." She looked up at Tobias.

He handed her his cell phone. "Call them." He kept the pistol pointed at the two thugs.

Elin dialed 112 and relayed all the information that the paramedics needed to know.

"They will be here as soon as possible. Whatever that means."

Tobias growled. "I have water in the car, it's in the door. Try to pour some in him."

Elin went back to the car and found the bottle. She first gave it to Maja, who gratefully took a big sip. Then Elin knelt down again beside Lars and put the bottle to his lips. Slowly she started to raise the bottle, the water flowed into his mouth. Lars coughed; his eyelids fluttered. He came to. He drank two sips of water, then he tried to sit up and moaned in pain.

"Lie still, Lars," Elin said. "The ambulance is on its way. We have everything under control."

Lars lay back down again. "Elin ..." he whispered. Elin bent over towards his face to be able to hear him better. "You... you have to check the cloud." He swallowed; Elin gave him another sip of water. "My cell phone is at the night club, in recording mode." He stared at her, then closed his eyes again.

"Got it," Elin replied. "We'll do that."

Lars seemed to lose consciousness again. Maja stood behind Elin and put a comforting hand on her shoulder. A siren could be heard in the distance.

It was Lisa who opened the door. Lars stood there with his arm in the sling and his disfigured face. He had looked at himself in the mirror earlier, so he was aware of what a sorry sight he made. They had patched him up in hospital, but the wounds remained. A broken rib, of course his nose, a moderate concussion, a muscle tear in his arm, a bruise on his ankle and countless small wounds from his tumble down the slope. He also had a memory lapse for about an hour. He still remembered that he had been put in Mehmed's car, but the drive and everything that had happened in the gravel pit had been completely erased. His memory only picked up again from the moment he woke up in the ambulance. But Elin had told him what had happened when they had talked on the phone that morning. It was difficult for him to smile at Lisa, every kind of facial expression hurt.

Lisa flinched. "Oh god, Lars, what happened?"

"Are you mad again?" he asked.

She shook her head. "Come in. Can I do anything to help?"

"It's okay." Slowly he limped into the living room and let himself sink carefully onto the couch. She looked down at him.

"Is there anything I can do? Looks like you've already been patched up. Do you want anything?"

"Something cold to drink, please."

"Okay." Lisa brought him a glass of water with ice cubes.

"So, tell me! What happened?"

"I was following a pimp. He noticed that and lured me into an ambush, they tied me up and then beat me up. If Elin and Maja hadn't shown up, they'd probably have killed me."

Lisa put her hand over her mouth. "Oh, no, how horrible."

Lars told her the whole story in detail, including his various diagnoses. "I don't know why this had to happen today of all days," he concluded. "Nothing like this has happened since we separated. And now that we've made up..."

"It's okay, Lars." She put her hand on his shoulder and kissed him gently on the cheek. "I learned my lesson."

He looked at her questioningly. "What do you mean?"

She looked him in the eye. "Well, I have always worried about everything. I believed that you shouldn't put yourself in danger, watched over the children like a mother hen and didn't take any risks myself. And? What good did that do? Now I have this disease, I am going to lose my breasts and I don't know how long I have to live... There is no point in being careful and worrying all the time. It may actually be harmful, because you tense up inside. Anyway, now I don't have much left to lose. I'll make the best of it. Your injuries will heal, as they always do, but my story probably won't go away so easily."

Lisa had really thought a lot, Lars was impressed. "The good news is I'm on sick leave for two weeks, so I'll be able to take care of the kids." Lars wanted to smile, but only ended up contorting his face. "The bad news is that my nose is broken, it will never look the same again."

"No problem, Lars. My breasts will soon be gone, which is much worse."

Lars swallowed. "Can't that be fixed with plastic surgery?"

"Yes, there are options available. We'll discuss them after I'm done with the entire treatment."

"I understand. And... ", he hesitated. "So, you're not angry with me for putting myself in a dangerous situation again?"

Lisa shook her head. "No, I'm sure you didn't do it on purpose, it's just something that can't be avoided in your line of work. No problem."

"Thanks, Lisa, I didn't expect this."

She took him in her arms, it felt so good. Why did Lisa have to get sick to come to this realization? They could have had it so much easier. Now all he could do was hope that she would get well again so that they would get another chance.

She let go of him and looked into his eyes. "I will take care of you this weekend. Starting Monday, I'll be at the hospital..."

"I know. Where are the kids?" He was surprised that they hadn't stormed in yet.

"They went to the supermarket to get rolls. We knew you were coming for breakfast. Although we didn't know in what condition. They'll be pretty shocked when they see you."

"Yeah, and then we have to give them another bit of shocking news regarding your treatment..."

Lisa nodded. "But I think we'll wait until tonight to do that."

"Agreed. Too much at once is never good. Plus, we still get to enjoy the day, so, I mean, you guys at least. I don't think I can do too much today. I'm supposed to rest today and tomorrow because of the concussion."

Lisa put her hand on his arm and smiled. She had tears in her eyes. It was a bit much for all of them to handle right now.

lin was still struggling from the events of the night, but nevertheless she pulled herself together, because Tobias had summoned her for 11 AM. Lars hadn't regained consciousness in the gravel pit, Elin had been very worried. Although the paramedics who drove him to the hospital said that all vital signs were okay. They suspected a concussion. After two more patrol cars arrived, the police took Mehmed and his gigantic buddy into custody. Mehmed couldn't walk properly; Maja must have hit him hard in the knee. He deserved it.

Afterwards, Elin and Maja had to give a first statement. So, they only got to bed at three o'clock. Elin had sent the taxi away after the police arrived. Tobias was nice enough to drive her and Maja home. After all, she had gotten to know a whole new side of Tobias yesterday. He was usually taciturn, always focused on work, and little interested in special jobs that could lead to potential employee downtime. Yesterday, on the other hand, he had been really cheerful, telling them that he had been in the military and was still active as a reserve officer. That explained his confident appearance in the gravel pit.

Elin opened the entrance door to the office with her access card and the corresponding code and marched straight into Tobias' office. He was already sitting in front of his PC.

"Hello Elin. Everything okay?"

She took a seat. "Yeah, no problem. Tired, but otherwise fine." She just had a few bruises. "Thanks again for yesterday. I'll never forget it. Lars was completely out of action. Maja and I were alone against these two guys, it would not have ended well."

Tobias nodded and grinned. "I almost enjoyed it a little. But I had the easy part, with the gun in my hand and all. For Lars the whole thing was certainly less amusing. Have you heard anything from him?"

"Yes, I spoke to him on the phone earlier when he was just released from the hospital. He has several wounds, but fortunately nothing serious. But he's on sick leave for two weeks."

Tobias pulled a face. "Typical, whenever you take on such special cases, there is always some downtime afterwards."

Elin looked at him angrily. Couldn't he think of anything else?

Tobias laughed and raised his hand. "I'm just kidding."

Elin exhaled strongly. Since when did Tobias make jokes?

"Look, this should interest you. Last night when I got home, I checked the cloud and found a long audio file that came from Lars' mobile phone. I listened to it right away. First there is a conversation between Lars and this Mehmed, but there is a lot of music in the background, so it's not easy to understand. But it was not very productive anyway, Lars asked about this Ali and if he had any problems. Mehmed didn't seem to like the topic, at least he quickly broke off the conversation. Shortly after that Lars is brought by someone else into a quiet room where there is a conversation with the head mobster. He asks Lars what he knows about Ali's death, and Lars says that the girl claims to be innocent and that there are indications that other people were present at the scene. Is that true?"

"He must have been bluffing. It's true about the girl, she talked about it for the first time yesterday, but Lars didn't know that yet. I told him only this morning, since I couldn't reach him yesterday."

"And the evidence?"

"None so far, that's just a hunch. However, the police haven't investigated everything either. If Hanna's statement is true, and I believe her, then there must have been someone else."

"Well, then I guess he really put his foot in his mouth with this bluff. Anyway, they got him out of the club afterwards." Tobias clicked with his mouse. "But after that it gets really interesting, there's a long pause, then this Mehmed comes back and talks to his boss."

"And you listened to this this morning? Without telling me?" Why did he keep it to himself for so long? He could have sent it to her.

"Yes, there is a problem. The conversation is in Arabic." Tobias smiled. "I'm not so good at it, are you?"

"Shit." Elin leaned back disappointed.

"So, this morning I contacted the translation agency we sometimes work with. For a small extra fee, they translated the interview for me immediately. I just got it in. Shall I read it?"

"Is there rice in China?" Elin grinned expectantly.

Tobias nodded. "Okay. Here we go:

– Boss, I got the car.

– Come in, close the door. Look, I want you to find out what he knows. I don't care what you have to do to get him to talk. Take him to the quarry. Nobody will hear you there.

– Okay, what do you want me to ask him?

– First, if he knows anything about the drugs. And then of course, if he can prove that we killed Ali.

– I did not kill Ali.

– I know that, Mehmed. But you were there. And you know that it had to be done. I was like a father to him. I helped him, you know, with the car and the apartment. I gave him stuff. And then he sells the competitor's drugs right here in my business. You don't bite the hand that feeds you. That had to be punished.

- But why did he have to die?

- He couldn't be counted on. Bad potatoes have to be sorted out or they all go bad. Traitors deserve to die. So, do you understand?

- Yes, I understand. Then what do we do with the snoop?

- You kill him. Best by using the stone press, that'll leave nothing behind. Here's the key.

- I'm not... I'm not killing anyone.

- Don't be such a pussy. I'll send the big guy with you. He'll do it.

- Thank you.

- All right. Get going."

Tobias paused. "What do you think?"

Elin was shocked, they had planned this from the beginning, Lars was actually supposed to die. "This is awesome. And that should be enough to exonerate Hanna."

"Yeah, I guess so. I'll email you the audio file and the translation, then you can forward it to the lawyer, or what do you think?"

"Absolutely. Anyway, I need to talk to him. He also doesn't know anything about Hanna's statement. I wanted to discuss it with Lars first, but he's out for now."

"That's right, you'll take the case now. Or what's left of it." Tobias smiled. "This app is good, right?"

"Yes, absolutely. Good thing Lars turned it on. Even though he almost paid for it with his life. If I hadn't happened to come to the nightclub that night, he wouldn't have had a chance."

"Fortune favors the brave." Tobias beamed. "Good work, Elin."

"Thank you." Another compliment. What was wrong with the boss? Did he have a new wife? Anyway, she liked this new Tobias much better than the old one. Hopefully he didn't fall back into his old ways at some point.

October 2018

37

It was the second working day after his sick leave. His foot was fine again, his nose and ribs were hardly in pain, and the wounds had formed scabs. The concussion had healed after a few days, so he was able to do the household chores with the children. Lisa was still in the hospital, and it probably would be another two weeks before she came home. The operation had been successful. So far everything was fine, even though Lisa was of course very unhappy about the way her body looked now. After the bandage was removed, she had asked him if he wanted to see it. Yes, he did. However, he had to promise her to put on his poker face, she didn't want to find pity or horror on his face. He thought he had done it reasonably well, but the sight had been frightening, they had indeed removed everything radically, only two scars remained.

Now it was time for the chemotherapy, and Lisa was feeling bad. After each infusion she was nauseous for hours, her hair had completely fallen out, she looked like a walking corpse. But she gritted her teeth and didn't complain. She was determined to beat the cancer.

The children were equally brave. They had been completely frightened when they heard about Lisa's illness, but by now they could handle it. Lars was in the hospital practically every day, at least for a short time, but he only took the children with him when he knew that Lisa was doing reasonably well, usually the day before the next infusion. At home things were not bad, the children went to school and he helped them with their homework. It was always in the evening, at bedtime, when the most difficult moment came. They wanted to know everything about Lisa and her condition, and Lars did his best to give them courage. He didn't have much to do with religion himself, but the children prayed every night, and of course Lisa's recovery was the greatest wish of all. He was touched every time they folded their little hands and asked the good Lord to let their mother get well quickly.

He had cleared everything with Tobias, he would now cut back a little, which meant no work in the evening and on weekends. On some days of the week, when one of the children had to leave school early, he could do his desk work from home. As soon as Lisa came out of the hospital, he would take a vacation. She would then still be very weak and would also have to continue the chemo with tablets, even if this should not be as bad as the therapy with the infusions.

The meeting today was very important, he would even have gone there while he was on sick leave or on vacation. Together with Elin he was at Edvard's office. The lawyer had announced that there was news.

"Yes, thanks again for your efforts. You have given the case a completely new twist, and the prosecution could not possibly ignore that. The police have reopened the investigation." Edvard took a break and looked at Lars. "I'm sorry that you have suffered such injuries. Still, I am glad that it turned out like that and not the way those guys had actually planned it. I cannot say it often enough - many thanks for your services. I will recommend you."

"That's good to hear," said Lars. Elin smiled satisfied.

"There is now a statement from Hanna." Edvard nodded at Elin. "Great that you finally got her to talk about what happened that day. Even better that she actually repeated it to the prosecutor's office."

Elin had to be there when the prosecutor questioned Hanna. She had asked her several times to tell the woman the same thing that she had already said in the conversation with her. Finally, Hanna had made up her mind to say a few sentences, and the prosecutor had been satisfied with that. After that, Hanna had withdrawn into herself again, and Elin had not been with her since then.

"Furthermore, we have the recording of the conversation between Mehmed and Najib; I am not sure if it will be admitted in court, since it was not done in a very official way. But the police played it for dear Mehmed, and he talked."

"Yes," shouted Elin.

Lars raised his eyebrows; he was curious to hear what the guy had said.

"As can already be seen from the conversation, this Najib apparently helped Ali to establish himself as a lover boy. He made the car available to him, brokered both the apartment in Sundbyberg and Botkyrka and apparently provided some kind of start-up financing. There was no exact repayment obligation for this, but Ali had to work for Najib and on the one hand had served in his club, on the other hand sold drugs and collected money. Probably it is extortion of protection money, that is not quite clear yet. Apparently, Ali then got involved with another drug dealer, but we don't know who specifically, and even sold his stuff in Najib's nightclub. When he was caught, Najib was pretty pissed and pulled him out of business for a night. From Sunday evening to Monday noon, Ali apparently was sitting in one of the rooms downstairs where you, Lars, were also held."

"But according to the autopsy report, the body had no other injuries," Lars objected. "The way they treated me, I would have expected that they would have given Ali a good going-over..."

Edvard shook his head. "I guess it wasn't that clear from the start what Ali was selling. This Najib only put out his feelers on Monday and then, when he finally had confirmation that Ali was really dealing for the competition, he coldly decided to dispose of him. Of course, they had confiscated Ali's cell phone, and Mehmed saw the text message from Hanna and told Najib about it, her intention to go to Tulegatan. Najib thought it was a great opportunity to blame the whole thing on poor little Hanna, which almost worked out. He told Ali that they would go to the apartment in Sundbyberg, and if everything was clean there, they would make a deal and forget the whole thing. Since Ali knew that there were no drugs in his apartment, he just ducked in there, he wasn't even tied up, according to Mehmed. In the apartment they timed the right moment, Najib stabbed Ali just before Hanna arrived there. Ali didn't suspect anything and must have been taken completely by surprise when Najib stabbed him out of the blue. They made a mess, wiped their fingerprints off and away they went."

The lawyer looked at them both. Lars wasn't exactly surprised, this Najib was a real gangster.

"What fucking thugs," cursed Elin.

"Yes, a wild story. There have been several arrests since then, Najib of course, but also several of his goons. They found traces of blood in the stone press in this gravel pit. It seems that these gorillas have misused this machine many times before. Who the victims were, however, is still completely unclear. The police recently conducted house searches at the nightclub and in the suspects' apartments. I'm sure they'll turn up something.

"My ID and phone - did that stuff show up anywhere?" Lars had a new phone in the meantime and his credit cards were all blocked, but he still had to get his ID card back. It was all very irritating.

"Your cell phone was found in the old town; the police were able to locate it. No fingerprints on it. Probably meant to look like you lost it. You'll get it back as soon as the police release it. The rest disappeared without a trace. Sorry."

Lars shrugged his shoulders; he hadn't given himself great hopes there anyway. "What about the crime scene in Tulegatan - did they find any traces?"

"Oh yes, right, on one of the pieces of broken glass was a fingerprint of the beast that was with you in the gravel pit, Micke is his name. He tried to wipe the glass but missed one."

"What does this mean for Hanna now?" Elin asked.

"Hanna is off the hook, of course. The prosecutor will drop the charges. The day after tomorrow is the hearing with the judge, I assume Hanna will be released immediately afterwards."

"Can I go there too?"

"Absolutely. I'll send you the time and place, and I'll see you there."

"Thank you."

Lars could understand that Elin wanted to be there, he himself didn't have such a great need for it, after all he had never met Hanna personally. But he was glad that the case had ended so well. It was to be hoped that this Najib and his henchmen would really be put behind bars, the outcome of such lawsuits was unfortunately never that easy to predict.

The lawyer thanked them again, asked them to send the final bill and accompanied them to the door.

"Are you pleased?" Lars asked Elin on the landing.

"Yes, I am glad Hanna is free. Mission completed. And I have to admit that I wasn't particularly optimistic at one point."

"True, it didn't look this good for a long time. We've been pretty much treading water. But as reward it went pretty fast in the end."

They took the elevator downstairs.

"How's Lisa?"

Lars had told Elin everything. "She is holding her own. But it's hard."

"Wish her the best from me, will you?"

"I will."

Downstairs they said goodbye. Lars had to go home. The little one had an early dismissal from school that day. If he hurried, he could just about make it to pick her up.

The trial progressed quickly. The prosecutor explained that she dropped the charges and had another suspect in custody who was charged with the crime. Evidence of this change of mind was briefly presented, then the judge determined that Hanna should be released immediately, even compensation for her time in custody was awarded. Edvard did not have to say a word.

Hanna was dressed better today than she had been during her incarceration, a blue sweatshirt and black jeans. Elin was sure Paula had brought these things for her. The girl seemed to be following the trial, but kept a straight face, even at the end when the acquittal was pronounced. Her parents, however, were cheering. They rushed straight to her and Paula hugged her, but Hanna hardly responded and did so awkwardly. The father shook the lawyer's hand, the couple had already thanked Elin outside in the corridor. They also asked her to give Lars a heartfelt thank you.

Elin did not want to intrude and waited until Hanna left the hall. But the girl ran straight along with one of the policemen.

"What happens now?" Elin wondered as the lawyer walked past her. "She is free, isn't she?"

"Absolutely, Hanna can leave right now, but she wants to get her things that are still in storage."

"Oh, I see." Elin decided to wait downstairs at the exit, she wanted to have a few words with Hanna. She said goodbye to Edvard, who had some other duties in the house.

Ten minutes later the Bergstrands came down the stairs. Hanna held her cell phone in front of her and stared at the screen, her mother supporting her by her elbow so she wouldn't stumble.

"Hello, Hanna." Elin took a few steps towards her.

The girl looked up, she was pale and without make-up. "Oh, hey."

"I'm glad you're free."

Hanna nodded absently.

"I just wanted to tell you, if you ever want to talk – here's my card. Feel free to call me, or we can get together sometime."

"Okay."

Hanna didn't move. Instead, Paula took the card. "Thanks, Elin. I'll keep it for Hanna and remind her of this."

"Good." Elin looked at Hanna somewhat irritated, the girl stared at her phone again. Elin peered over the edge – a picture of Hanna and Ali, up on a roof in the evening sun, both laughing all over their faces. That was what was so important, she had missed the pictures in prison, of course. Nevertheless, Elin had hoped that Hanna had gained some distance to Ali in the last weeks, but apparently this was not the case.

"Okay, then you'd better take your daughter home again. All the best."

The parents thanked her and said *"hejdå"*. Elin watched the three of them leave the building through the big glass door.

She fervently hoped that Hanna would succeed in freeing herself from this time with her loverboy.

39

She got up and checked her phone, yes, it was fully charged. She put on her jacket and walked out of her room. Her mother sat in the living room and did a crossword puzzle. She looked up.

"Are you going out?", she asked astonished.

Hanna nodded. "I have made some plans to meet Klara", she lied.

Her mother got up and smiled. "I'm glad. That'll do you good. Come here." She took Hanna in her arms.

Hanna put her arms around her waist. "Thanks, Mama. For everything."

"But, my dear daughter, that goes without saying. You'll see, everything will be fine. It just takes a little time. And you meeting up with Klara is a good first step. I'm sure you'll get along fine again."

Hanna nodded and slowly released herself.

"Take care, Mama."

"Yeah, and you as well. See you later." Her mother looked at her thoughtfully. Hanna turned around and quickly left the apartment. The elevator came immediately. As she stepped out the front door, she looked around for Ali's car. It was a reflex, the car couldn't be here, Ali was no longer alive. The pain was deep and the habit of looking for his car only made it worse. She gulped.

She walked slowly but surely to the subway station. She had to wait ten minutes for the next train to Solna, today on Sunday the schedule was not very busy. She had never taken the subway with Ali, always in his Audi. She fought back the tears again. She knew he hadn't loved her as much as she loved him, but that didn't change her own feelings. She missed him terribly. The ten days she'd been home had been unbearable. In prison they had at least left her alone, now someone was constantly annoying her - her sister, her parents. Everyone tried to cheer her up, persuade her to do something. She was so fed up with it. At least they had granted her a grace period last week, she had been able to stay home, but tomorrow she was supposed to go back to school. Everybody would be all over her, asking questions, looking stupid, wanting something from her again ... she couldn't do it.

She got off at the second station, Sundbyberg Center. There was little activity on the platform, she went up the escalator and took the exit Stationsgatan. From there it was a good ten minutes to walk. Should she hurry or just stroll along? She didn't know, it didn't really matter. The important thing was that she had made up her mind. She knew what she wanted.

She did not notice much of her surroundings; she had passed the church and finally she was standing in front of the house. The code didn't work, they had probably changed it. Of course, she could not ring his doorbell, she looked at the sign, his name was no longer there. But she was lucky, someone had just come out of the elevator and opened the front door. She slipped in and took the elevator up. As she passed the eighth floor, the tears came, she couldn't hold them back anymore.

Finally, the elevator stopped. She got out, everything was a blur, but through the veil of tears she recognized the stairs leading to the roof. Slowly she climbed up. She stopped in front of the metal door. She reached for the door frame. Yes, the key was still there. She unlocked the door and pushed it open to the outside. It was windy up here, she let her hair flutter. The door slammed shut behind her.

Hanna stood on the platform and looked over the rooftops of the other houses. Tears were flowing, the dam had burst. She thought of the first time she had been up here with Ali. How he had held her in his arms, she had felt so safe. And then his kisses... It would never be like that again. She reached into her bag and pulled out a cigarette. She turned her back against the wind to light it. She drew intensely on the cigarette, she wanted to get back the memory of how they had smoked here together. But Ali was not there, the cigarette didn't taste good. She dragged on it twice more, then she put it out. Everything was over.

She looked at her beautiful ring and twisted it around her finger. Then she took out her smartphone from her purse. Five missed calls from her mother. Good thing she had it turned down. She opened her photo album. Pictures of her and Ali and of Ali by himself. How she loved his smile. Such happy moments. She wiped the tears from her eyes, she wanted to look at the photos again. One picture after the other, even if it hurt. She paused at one of the pictures they had taken up here - one of her favorite pictures. They both smiled into the camera, she leaned against him, the evening sun bathed her in a golden light. Hanna forced herself to look at the other photos as well. Ali, who smiled at her. Hanna pressed the phone to her lips and kissed Ali's picture. Eventually she had reached the end. The end in a two-fold sense.

She had thought it over and over for the past week. What was left for her? Nothing made sense. She knew that her parents would be sad. But they couldn't take any pleasure in the Hanna that she was now. Without the energy of life, without the joy of living. Besides, they'd still got Evelina, she was almost always in a good mood. There was nobody else who'd miss her. It was the right decision.

Slowly, she walked up to the edge of the roof.

40

lin was sitting next to Maja in the car when the call came. They had been in Sigtuna for Sunday brunch. Maja had to give two lessons in the studio that morning, then they had left. The food was great, and the view of the Mälaren Bay was fantastic, the sun was reflected on the water. After having coffee, they headed down to the lake and strolled along the shore, arm in arm. It had been a bit windy, but they had enjoyed it. On the right the water and on the left Sigtuna with the beautiful houses on the hillside.

They were already on the highway, just before Kista. Elin saw on the display that it was Paula, Hanna's mother. What did she want?

"Hello?"

"Elin?"

"Yes."

"This is Paula. Sorry, I... I didn't know who else to call." She sounded out of breath.

"Did something happen?"

"I don't know, I have such a bad feeling. Hanna left earlier; I was so happy because she wanted to meet Klara. But when she was gone, I got worried, she said goodbye in such a strange way. So, I called Klara to tell her to be nice to Hanna. But Klara didn't know about any plans. Now I'm afraid Hanna will hurt herself. She doesn't answer her phone."

Elin wondered. "How has she been lately? Did she get somewhat better?"

"No, not at all. She can't be persuaded to do anything. Just sits in her room, hardly eats. That's why I was so surprised she wanted to see Klara. It was the first time she wanted to do something on her own. I ran after her, but she was already gone."

"And you have no idea where she went?"

"No, she has no one else. I've already called her grandmother. I don't know where to look for her. Do you have an idea?"

Elin wondered. "Maybe she went to Ali's apartment?"

"But why? Ali is dead. She doesn't even have a key."

"Yes, but there are a lot of memories there. And if you think she's planning on hurting herself..." Elin thought about the roof, she knew that Ali had often been there with her, Hanna had spoken about it in prison. "Paula, we are not far from the house, we'll go there. I'll call you back."

"Thanks, Elin. I hope you find her."

Elin could still hear Paula sobbing before she hung up. She turned to Maja: "We have to go to Sundbyberg, Tulegatan. Hanna may be there and want to harm herself." She briefly recounted what had happened.

Maja nodded. "Okay, what's the best way to go? Solna exit?"

"No, there can be a lot of traffic, take the E18 and from there to Sundbyberg. And as fast as you can."

Again, Maja nodded, she accelerated. "Do you think she wants to jump off the roof?"

"If she wants to end things, that would be an obvious possibility. That way she can feel close to Ali one last time and reminisce."

"She should have gotten over him by now, shouldn't she?"

"You'd think so, but I think she never stopped loving him. And she doesn't seem to have the energy to start over."

"I see. But how did she get in there and then up on the roof?"

"Well, you know you can always get in the house. I don't know how to get to the roof, maybe it's unlocked."

Luckily there was not much traffic, after a quarter of an hour they were at the house, Maja stopped in second row. "You start running. I'm looking for a parking space. And be careful that you don't fall down with her."

Elin grunted and jumped out of the car. The entrance was between two restaurants, the pizzeria and an Asian one. Arriving at the entrance, she pulled at the door - locked, of course. She pressed her hands on all the bells at once. Someone would open it.

When nothing happened, she pressed again. Finally, she heard several voices at the same time.

"Pizza service," she called out. Even though several answered that they hadn't ordered anything, one seemed to have mercy and pressed the door opener. Elin tore open the door and ran inside, the elevator was fortunately available. It took what felt like ten minutes before the door finally closed and the elevator started moving. At least it was much faster than if she had to run up the stairs to the ninth floor. Apart from the fact that she would then hardly have any breath left once she got to the top. She could only hope that she wasn't too late.

The elevator finally came to a stop, she squeezed through the doors before they were fully open and looked around. Another small staircase, then a heavy metal door. The key was in the door, so it was as simple as that. She threw herself against the door and jumped onto the flat roof. Yes, that's where Hanna stood, right on the edge. Her long hair fluttering in the wind.

"Hanna!" shouted Elin softly.

Hanna turned and stared at her. Her face was expressionless.

"Hanna, what are you doing? Come back! Let me hug you." Slowly Elin walked towards her.

Hanna shook her head.

"You have your whole life ahead of you. Don't throw it away! You're so young, everything can be solved." Elin took two more steps; it was only a few feet further to Hanna. "I'll help you too."

Hanna spread her arms.

"Hanna, please, let's talk." Elin's voice became more and more insistent.

But Hanna said nothing, she closed her eyes.

"No!" Elin screamed and jumped into action.

But it was too late, Hanna let herself fall backwards over the edge. Elin missed her by a yard, she had to brake to avoid falling down herself. She could see Hanna fall before her body hit the ground with an awful sound. A woman with a baby carriage cried out in horror down the street. Elin saw a pool of blood spreading under Hanna. She knelt down and hammered her fist on the roof.

"Damn it! No, no, no." She pulled her head back and sat on the roof. She had come too late. Should she have handled it differently? What could have stopped Hanna? She held her hands in front of her face, tears rushed from her eyes. What a tragedy.

The door to the stairs behind her opened, Maja came out onto the roof.

"Isn't she here?"

Elin looked up at her and took a deep breath. "Not anymore, she just jumped. I could not stop her. One moment she was still standing there, the next moment she was gone," she exclaimed.

"Oh no." Maja came to her, crouched down and hugged her. "I'm so sorry."

A loud scream could be heard from below, Elin and Maja looked down over the edge. Hanna's mother stood in front of the house and held her hands in front of her mouth. She stared at her daughter's dead body. The woman with the baby carriage was on the phone, hopefully with the emergency call. A man stood next to her and filmed.

Elin became angry. "Stop filming, you idiot", she screamed from the roof, but the man didn't let go. She had no illusions that the scene with Hanna's dead body in the puddle of blood would be on the net and go around the world in a few minutes.

She pointed at Paula and swallowed. "That's Hanna's mother. Apparently, she also made her way here after our conversation. She also came too late. Shit." At least she didn't have to give her the bad news, she thought, but she immediately reprimanded herself for this thought. It would have been better if Paula had been spared this sight.

Maja wiped the tears from Elin's face and pulled her up. "Let's go. There's nothing more we can do."

"You're right. But why did it have to end this way? What did we stand up for? She could have stayed in prison. She couldn't have killed herself there."

"Oh, you know that if you really want to, you can do it anywhere. And your efforts have at least caught the real killer."

"Yeah, at least that." Elin nodded resignedly. That didn't really comfort her. "Maybe I should have looked after her more. We had a good relationship." Elin regretted that she had not contacted her since Hanna's release.

Maja shook her head and sighed. "Elin, you can't take responsibility for everything. You helped her get out of prison. You offered her the chance to meet you. She clearly didn't want that."

"Maybe she didn't have the courage. I could have at least called her and asked."

"You're a private investigator, not a psychologist. I don't think meeting you would have solved Hanna's problems either. Elin, really, your job was finished. I mean, I think it's great that you're still visiting that little girl Ebba, and I'm sure you've made an important contribution, but you can't do that for every one of your clients - you can't do it in terms of time or mentally, not to mention that you're not getting paid for it."

"Yeah, you're probably right."

"I most certainly am. Ask Lars."

"I know." Elin straightened up and headed for the door with Maja. "Why did she love that bastard so much?"

Maja turned her palm upwards. There was probably no answer for that.

EPILOGUE

November 2018

41

ars was heading home; he had been out shopping. Now, he was looking forward to having breakfast with Lisa. She had still been asleep when he got up, but by now she was most certainly awake. She was doing much better at the moment than she had been in the hospital. She was in the final cycles of her chemotherapy, and she tolerated the tablets much better than the infusions. The doctors had been right about that. Although she was usually nauseous for a while after taking the pills, that quickly passed. In the hospital, on the other hand, she had puked her guts out. Of course, she was weak and had become thin, but she joked about it and said it was the first diet that actually worked.

Lars parked his Volvo in the driveway and fetched the two bags from the trunk. Lisa opened the door and smiled at him.

"Good morning, honey."

"Lisa, go inside so you don't catch a cold." He quickly put down one of the bags and closed the door behind him. She stood there with the woolen beanie covering her bald head and wearing her tight athletic clothes; she had started to work out since she was at home. It had been recommended that she do so. It seemed that there was new evidence from a Swedish study that a combination of strength training and intensive interval training reduced side effects, such as fatigue and weakness. While in the hospital Lisa was not feeling well enough for it, but now she felt that it was good for her. Lars had brought the indoor bike up from the basement and placed it in one of the corners of the living room, they also had various dumbbells and resistance bands, so Lisa could train for a while every morning.

"I've already made coffee," she said while setting the table as Lars unpacked the bags.

"Greetings from Elin." She had called him this morning on his way to the supermarket. "The prosecutor brought charges against the entire gang of criminals. The evidence against them is said to be solid."

The police had obviously done a good job this time. They had analyzed the cell phone data of Mehmed, Najib and the giant Micke and were able to match the movement patterns with Mehmed's statement. All three had been in Tulegatan at the time of the crime. In addition, two witnesses had been found who had seen the three of them arrive in two cars together with Ali and enter the house that day. Furthermore, they were charged with the attempted murder of Lars, which meant that they would all have to testify in court.

"That's good, our city will be a little safer." Lisa poured the coffee. "How is her awareness campaign doing?"

Elin had been very frustrated after Hanna's suicide. Lars couldn't imagine how Elin could have prevented it, but Elin just couldn't dismiss what had happened. She had pointed out to him, "Lars, we have solved the case, but we couldn't save the victim." That was true, of course, but neither had they taken responsibility for Hanna's ultimate fate. Many crimes involved victims who suffered permanent injuries or severe trauma, these were not the kind of problems that a private detective could solve. For this there were parents, relatives, friends, doctors and psychologists. But no matter what he told Elin; she would not be content. And so, she had been interviewed by a newspaper reporter about the phenomenon of loverboys in general and Hanna's tragic case in particular. The interview had been done with the consent of Hanna's parents, and Tobias had also permitted it. So, this time Elin had actually full permission - something Lars smiled about, because otherwise she usually acted first and asked later when everyone was angry, or it was too late anyway. In any event, this interview had led to inquiries from many schools, and they invited Elin to speak to their teenage girls about it.

"It got off to a good start, she has already been to two schools and has generated a lot of interest. Now she is even going to be on TV."

Lisa sat with him. "I'm glad. She's really turning your case into something positive after all."

Lars nodded. He also liked what Elin was doing, even if he had some doubts about how she would manage to reconcile all of this, both in terms of time and spirit. Elin continued to visit little Ebba also, and if there was someone to look after the next case, Elin would soon be fully booked. However, Tobias had approved all of Elin's activities, even during working hours, which really surprised Lars. In the past, Tobias had had his doubts about Elin from the start; he had long refused to let her leave the office and do detective work. And besides that, he had always been opposed to everything that did not directly bring in money. But since that joint operation in the gravel pit, he was like a different person. He was friendly, supported Elin in everything and even handed out compliments. Inwardly, Lars shook his head about this change, but it was for the better, so he wouldn't complain. It was also great that they now had a third person in the company who they could count on when it mattered.

Lisa sat beside him and stroked his face. "Well, slowly but surely your many small wounds are healing. Only your nose is a little bit wider now. But it suits you."

"Thank goodness." His nose was still sore, but he had come to terms with the new shape.

"You know, I've been thinking, it's always you who ends up getting hurt the most in these dangerous situations."

Lars thought about that. Yes, that was true, in almost all of these situations where it came to violent confrontations, he took the lion's share of the beating. Elin, for example, got off much easier each time. What was Lisa's point?

She smiled. "Don't worry. I don't think it is a bad omen or anything like that. And you are definitely just as good in these fights as the others. I think you have a protective instinct; you stick up for yourself with everything you've got, and you stick up for others as well, and especially for others."

Lisa stroked his neck. "And that's a wonderful quality, truly lovable. I know that if it ever came down to it, you'd fight the same way for the kids or for me."

Lars looked into her eyes. "I thought I was doing that right now." He put his arms around her. "Even if in a different way..."

"That's right, you do." Lisa put her forehead against his. "I'm so grateful to you, I don't know how I'd get through all of this without you, in every respect."

Lars closed his eyes. Yes, that was his duty. Elin should continue her campaign, that was good. She had asked him if he wanted to participate too, but he had Lisa, who needed him a lot now. And two girls who would also soon be teenagers. He wanted to do everything he could to ensure that they had a solid home and an intact family, and to give them so much security and self-confidence that they wouldn't even give a guy like Ali the time of day.

He could do that. That was the most important thing for him - his family.

And of course, he was a private detective, but that was all he was.

Your Free Book

Read the Prequel to the Stockholm Sleuth Series

A short crime story about Lars, one of the private eyes in the series. In this story he is still working as a policeman.
Together with his partner Kalle, Lars is called to a house where neighbours report a quarrel.
This case will change Lars' career forever.

*Exclusive short story for readers of the series –
download here:*

www.christertholin.one/free

Thanks to the reader

I am thrilled that you have chosen my book.

I am even more thrilled that you have read it to the end. I especially hope that you liked it. If so, I would like to ask you for a small favour: take a few moments of your time and rate my book on Amazon. Your help in spreading the word is gratefully appreciated and **reviews** make a huge difference to helping new readers find the series.

You can also let me know directly what you thought about the book! Your feedback is extremely important to me – this way I get the chance to consider the preferences of my readers.

contact@christertholin.one
www.christertholin.one

My heartfelt thanks
Christer Tholin

About the author

The author is originally from Schleswig-Holstein in Germany and has lived for many years with his family in Stockholm / Sweden, where he works as an independent management consultant.

He is a great fan of Swedish crime literature and had been planning for a long time to make his own contribution. That has already come to fruition with his first book, VANISHED? which is also the first book of the *Stockholm Sleuth Series* introducing Elin and Lars. SECRETS? is their second case and MURDER? the third.
www.christertholin.one

VANISHED?

Stockholm Sleuth Series, Book 1
By Christer Tholin
2016, Stockholm

She: a very hot 30 something Swedish woman. ***He:*** a native of Berlin, on vacation in rural Sweden, seeking solace for his broken heart. They meet. He finds her irresistible. But before their relationship can get off the ground, she vanishes mysteriously, having apparently been abducted. So Martin sets out to rescue Liv from her captors, with the aid of two Swedish detectives in a race against time – and across Sweden. In so doing, Martin and his intrepid detective duo put their very lives on the line.

https://www.amazon.com/gp/product/B071KYQ2XZ/

SECRETS?

Stockholm Sleuth Series, Book 2
By Christer Tholin
2017, Stockholm

In the crime novella SECRETS?, fledgling private investigator Elin
Bohlander takes on what looks like an easy assignment — at first:
to determine if her client's boyfriend is having an affair with
another woman. To do this, Elin follows him to a secluded cabin in
the woods, where she soon discovers that what's actually
transpiring is stranger than anyone thought. Having ventured too
far, she's stumbled upon a hornet's nest and put her life at risk. But
it's too late. Can Elin win the unequal fight against a gang of brutal
child molesters?

https://www.amazon.com/gp/product/B075VWXGHN/

MURDER?

Stockholm Sleuth Series, Book 3
By Christer Tholin. 2019, Stockholm

Christina's idyllic existence with her husband Patrik comes to an abrupt end when Patrik suddenly vanishes from their suburban home in Stockholm. Christina is precipitated into a hellishly desperate and anguished search for Patrik – which after six weeks turns up nary a trace of him.

At her wits end, she contacts local sleuths Lars and Elin, who, after a brief investigation, reach the conclusion that Patrik simply decided to abandon his cushy existence to embark on a new life – without Christina.

Lars and Elin ultimately trace Patrik's movements to the wooded wilds of northern Sweden, but too late – he's found dead. The police rule his death an accident, but Christina thinks otherwise – and so she asks Lars and Elin to do a thorough investigation of the circumstances surrounding Patrik's demise. Was his death really accidental, or was foul play involved? And was the mysterious Natalia somehow implicated?

Unfortunately, none of the countless leads that Lars and Elin follow up gets them any closer to solving the mystery of Patrik's death. But then they get a startling break that results in Christina having to make a tricky and extremely consequential decision that plunges our three protagonists into a life or death struggle.

https://www.amazon.de/dp/B07JBNJCH3/